Extravaganza

S. J. Riccobono

Order this book online at www.trafford.com
or email orders@trafford.com

Most Trafford titles are also available at major online book retailers.

Printed in Victoria, BC, Canada.

ISBN: 978-1-4269-2551-1 (sc)

*Our mission is to efficiently provide the world's finest, most comprehensive
book publishing service, enabling every author to experience success.
To find out how to publish your book, your way, and have it available
worldwide, visit us online at www.trafford.com*

Trafford rev. 02/10/2010

 www.trafford.com

North America & international
toll-free: 1 888 232 4444 (USA & Canada)
phone: 250 383 6864 ♦ fax: 812 355 4082

2047

WHAT WAS ONCE PARADISE LOST was earth renewed. If the world had been imperfect and yet remained beautiful; how much more could artificial perfection bring ultimate success? Corruptive forces had been eradicated, replaced by a pristine ecosystem where all could enjoy the fullness of life. Blue skies, brilliant clouds and a dust free atmosphere smelled as clean and fresh as if it had been created moments ago. Turquoise lakes and calm glassy oceans surrounded landscapes rich with colorful flowers and thick green trees. The days and nights were tempered and the tiniest dew drop had its moment of glory before melting away. Endless farmlands rolled over lazy valleys and coiffed gardens decorated every city. Decay was a burden of the past and every molecule was constantly identified and regulated. Nothing on earth was left to chance.

With the exception of domestic cats and dogs, most animal and insect life was considered unnecessary. Doctors, medicine, lawyers and tradesmen were history; remnants of a regrettable past. The monumental cities were expansive metallic giants climbing high above sidewalks void of garbage or debris. Flying vehicles silently flew between glistening towers, transporting overly polite passengers to their various locations.

The neighborhoods were manicured wonderlands that fed off the city centers. Rows and rows of quaint houses with blue grass yards and public parks provided families with everything they needed. Children played in the streets while adults sauntered peacefully amidst the scented air of sweet nectar and buttery popcorn.

Wherever people gathered, they treated each other with respect and dignity.

In the suburbs vehicles hovered in and out of the lush neighborhoods, often landing on the front lawns. When father came home from work he walked cheerfully up the brick path and was greeted by his adoring children, who leaped up into his waiting arms, and then his wife, who pecked him on the cheek. Inside the house they gathered around the dinner table and told stories about their fascinating exploits.

The next day father and mother woke up with a smile and father sprayed the front lawn with a garden hose. He greeted his next door neighbor, who was doing the same. "Hello Jim. A good morning to you."

"Thanks Bill."

"Taking the kids to the mountains today?"

"If that's what they want."

"Yes, anything they want."

"And how is your wife?"

He grinned from ear to ear. "As good a woman as one could ever dream of. I'm sure you feel the same about yours?"

"She's faultless."

"I bet it's going to be a good golf day?"

"I'm counting on it."

"Your usual 68?"

"That's my score every time."

They simultaneously ducked back into their houses.

Mother gathered the children to go ice skating on the lake. It was sunny and warm, but technology provided ice at a moment's notice. They put on their skates and each maneuvered like professionals with leaps and twirls abound. No one ever stumbled or injured themselves and all the mothers shouted supportively from the lake's edge.

"So Jeanne, how's your day going?"

"Fine, Ann. And how about you, Irene?"

"Excellent. I love my life."

"I can't wait to go home to my husband."

"I know how you feel. My husband is so perfect."

"Mine, too. Aren't husbands the greatest?"

"Yes they are. And we have the most delightful families."

"I hear you're going to visit your mother next week?"

"She wants to see the children."

"Will she take them to the park?"

"Yes, they have a nice park where she lives."

"Good. My parents want our kids to visit, too."

"That's a good idea."

"Things are good, Irene. Really good."

The calls of noisy children echoed across neighborhood streets as they popped in and out of each other's houses. Games like hide and go seek and tag were regular daily events; and nobody cared who won or lost. Long gone were the days of heartless competition that might crush the soul of a sensitive youth. Kids were nice to each other too; not mean like they used to be.

During the soothingly seventy degree nights, baseball games took place at every park. Hundreds of ordinary folks sat in bleachers and shouted praise for their favorite teams. Coaches were kind and spoke only encouraging words and parents bragged about their own family, as well as their neighbors. Hot dogs and french fries were eagerly devoured and ice cream cones dripped down the sides of clasping hands. The first batter up adjusted her cap, the catcher signaled with downward pointing fingers and the pitcher threw a ball that was hit for a home run.

"Way to go, Millie!"

"You go for it, girl!"

When the score was tied in the later innings, most kids were satisfied and wanted to call off the game. The tasty ice cream was more alluring than a final victory. Afterwards gentle breezes beckoned families to the center of the park to listen to live music and float along a lake in paddleboats that barely stirred the waters. It was this way all around the world. Everyone lived in prosperity and treated one another lovingly.

In the latter hours of the evening, mother and father sat in reclining chairs between a small table and softly lit lamp as the fireplace blazed and the children slept. Father read his book and mother knitted her quilt. The cat leaped up on father's lap and the dog slept at mother's feet.

"What should we do tomorrow, dear?"

"It's up to you, my love."

She sighed comfortably. "Oh, you're so good to me."

Father put down his book as the cat's tail swiped against his arm. "Life is so perfect. And it will be like this forever."

April 2020

Taxed and taxed and taxed again, the American people had nothing more to give. They were tired of paying for war, paying for peace, paying for other people's problems and fighting for the dwindling resources that remained. The once great nation of the United States was broken and it was difficult to maintain order. The popular chants of the day were secession; and states like Texas, Nevada, Montana, Wyoming and Florida had already done so. Washington D. C. was still the seat of government, but politicians and generals found their worldly influence dwindling by the day. Local police forces were overwhelmed by criminals and roving gangs and all government services were harder to come by. This was not the America the founding fathers had envisioned.

California was unmanageable and considered dangerous. New York City was a war zone and other eastern cities didn't fare much better. Nevada, now governed by its own leaders, had a well organized infrastructure and police force. It was even rumored that some of its citizens kept private nuclear arsenals. Whatever the truth, Nevada was a state to be envied. Las Vegas was still a popular playground for the wealthy, but a new location emerged in the desert that attracted visitors from all over the world. Unlike the Las Vegas strip, where the once fancy veneers lost its luster, the hotel Extravaganza boasted of five star accommodations, a lavish casino, its own water reclamation system and small nuclear reactor to supplement its power source. Just off the famous extraterrestrial highway, it was even reported to possess an authentic UFO film that was available to those that could afford the price of admission.

Where other hotels were often decrepit and empty, Extravaganza was always booked. It had one of the most elite security teams for the protection of the guests. Harry Philer, the co-owner along with his silent partners of dubious reputations, operated a shiny metallic oasis in the middle of the most inhospitable surroundings. Harry was a stout sixty year old man with thousand dollar suits and satin ties; sparing no expense on jet helicopters, jet aircraft and mint condition automobiles. While presenting himself as royalty, his personal habits did not equal his image. He sat in his office behind an eighteenth century desk, chewing peanuts and spitting out tiny chunks while dictating a letter to his secretary.

"Tell the butcher he sent me sub-standard meat last month. I pay good money for the best. If I want dog meat, I'll go to Vegas."

"Will that be all, sir?"

He leaned back and choked on a bit of husk. "I'm expecting some important guests in a couple of days. Make sure everything's all right."

"Everything has been taken care of."

"Good, because I've buried people who didn't follow my orders. Now I'm talking about you, of course."

She seemed dismissive. "Yes, Mr. Philer."

"I want to talk security. Send in Blake."

She left the room and five minutes later Melanie Blake, a red haired beauty entered his office in a drab gray business suit and white blouse. She was thirty five years of age and had been a former elite employee of the Federal Bureau of Investigation. She now had the title of chief of security and oversaw the guards, the underground missile silos and the safety of all the guests.

"Sit down, Melanie. Peanuts?"

"No thanks."

"The big six are coming in two days."

"So I've heard."

He winked. "Don't be a smart ass."

She brushed her silky bangs to the side. "Thursday, 4:15 in the afternoon by helicopter."

"These guys helped build this hotel, so I want everything spiffed up."

"No worries, Harry."

"They'll pay for two months expenses."

"They've already sent their bodyguard rosters and security needs."

He scratched his crotch without embarrassment. "I want to show them a good time. I'm relying on you."

"Have I ever let you down?"

"No, you're the best." He salaciously eyed her. "Tell me Blake, what do you do for fun?" The rest of the staff have their little trysts. Even Matheson enjoys his boys. What about you?"

She swaggered over to him, hips jutting side to side. Mouth agape, he held back peanut particles from sliding off the tip of his tongue. She walked around behind him, leaned over and straightened his tie. "I appreciate the concern, Harry. But I never mix business with pleasure. I find it much easier to rely on electricity. It always leaves me satisfied." She stood up straight and walked out of the room with a smile on her face.

Harry mumbled quietly. "I'd like be your batteries."

At twelve midnight a group of tourists eagerly waited in line along the side of the casino where a parked bus opened its doors. A man in a blue uniform called out to them. "Have your tickets ready. If you don't have tickets, they're still selling tickets at the box office."

Anticipating the journey, the guests bantered relentlessly as they swarmed the bus, took their seats and read the brochures. The doors closed and two black security vans parked in front and behind the bus. Upon departure, the uniformed man stood by the driver with a microphone. "Welcome ladies and gentlemen to the Extravaganza UFO tour. We'll be driving about twenty minutes on the highway and then we'll take a side road to our destination. We can not guarantee a sighting every night, but more than often we have some kind of activity. Enjoy the trip, and please remain in your seats while we're in motion."

The black vans each carried a contingency of six armed personnel. The bus and its escorts seem to be alone on the highway, passing only one car. The convoy steered onto the smaller side road and twisted up the canyon. Five minutes later the air brakes hissed and the bus came to an abrupt stop. "Ladies and gentlemen, we may have an encounter. Please exit in an orderly fashion and stay behind the guard rails. We just may get lucky."

They eagerly disembarked and the bus driver

pointed to a faint light on a far ridge. "There, along the cliff. It could be aliens."

The flash of light intensified and the guests stretched their necks out. It was extremely bright and danced across the cliff until it disappeared. "That might have been a UFO. Too bad we weren't closer. Maybe it's still around. Let's get into the bus and continue up the road."

Unbeknownst to the tourists, a man several hills away sat next to an outbuilding and chewed on a jelly sandwich and sipped from a soda can. He controlled a powerful searchlight which had just strafed the hillside to create the fascinating illusion. The tourists pressed their faces against the windows for a glimpse of a flying saucer. The bus stopped again and everybody ran out the doors. The guide spoke in whispers. "Ladies and gentlemen, I've just been informed that there's activity reported in the area. If everyone remains calm, we may encounter it."

The crowd hushed and surveyed the dark skies above he ridgeline. They gasped in amazement when a bright ball of light rose over the hills. It stopped, reconfigured into a flying disc and flew smoothly across the sky. It vanished and left a blue residual cloud of light; which also dissipated. "Ladies and gentlemen, that was a rare treat. To see one so close. How incredible. Only a few guests have had such a close encounter. Well, that's why we call it the UFO highway. We can now return to the hotel. Please watch your step getting back inside."

The bus drove away and two men operating a holographic power mirror shut down their machinery for the night and crept back into their bunker where they would sleep during the day. Although initially expensive, ticket sales had already paid for most of the technological gadgetry.

Melanie Blake made her early morning rounds through the casino floor. The gambling traffic was light as most guests were still up in their rooms. Holding onto a cup of coffee, she stopped in front of an inconspicuous door, tapped in her special code and entered the hotel's security center. As she passed by rows of computer terminals and monitoring stations, her employees all greeted her enthusiastically.

She walked into her office and ran over to answer the ringing phone. "Yes? Oh yes, send him in."

Two security guards escorted a thirty year old man up to her desk.

"Please be seated, Mr. Humphries."

He sat down across her nervously. "What's this all about?"

She smiled. "I think you know what this is about. You've been cheating."

"Whaa…what do you mean?"

She activated a wall monitor. "This is you at the craps table. Palming chips is an old, tired practice. I have to admit, you're pretty good at it." She drew her finger on her desktop. "You picked the wrong establishment, Mr. Humphries. Harry Philer owns this place. Have you ever heard of him?"

He tried acting cool. "Yeah, I think so."

"Out here, he's the law, judge and jury. It's a big desert and from my vantage point you're heading for a hole out there."

"What can I do to fix this?"

"Tell you what, pay us back twice what you took from us and we'll let you go."

"I can't get that kind of money."

"Not our problem. We'll take Euros transferred to us in two days."

"And if I can't do that?"

"You may simply seize to exist."

He grinned nervously. "You'll get your payment."

"I thought so. Now these men will escort you back to your room. And I hope you don't mind if they baby-sit you?"

She reviewed her schedule and then retired to a state of the art gymnasium where she changed into her sweats. She waited patiently on the mat until a muscular man approached her and smacked his fists together. He bowed, folded his hands in a martial arts gesture and then rushed her; only to be tripped and thrown down to the floor. He leaped up and roundhouse kicked her, but she sidestepped him and then threw two quick punches. She kicked him twice, swung her foot under his leg and toppled him to the mat.

"That's the best you got?"

"I'm stronger, you're faster."

"I need better competition to keep me on my toes."

He snickered, and then brushed himself off. "Then you'll just have to import it. Because I'm the best you got."

"Bring in two of your best fighters."

Without warning two guards charged her from opposite directions. Fists and legs flying, she swiveled right and left and knocked both of them to the mat.

A third guard wrapped his arms around her back, but with one leg she stepped back between his legs and then flipped him over her. Melanie bowed to them and wiped a drop of blood off her nose. "Had enough?"

The head guard nodded. "We're going to the showers."

It was late afternoon and the hazy orange sun baked one side of the hotel's windows. Twin helicopters thundered over low hills on approach to an exterior tarmac where a multitude of neatly organized guards with assault rifles were poised to greet them. Harry and Melanie stood between the human gauntlets as the helicopter blades whipped their hair and clothes.

The pilots landed the craft, shut down the engines and three well dressed men and their personal guards emerged from each helicopter. All wore dark sunglasses as they moved towards Harry, who vigorously shook their hands. "Gentlemen, gentlemen, good to see you. You all know my chief of security, Melanie Blake. She will take you to your rooms and see to your needs."

They politely nodded and followed her and the guard detail into the hotel where they boarded a private elevator to their penthouse rooms. Each was given a luxurious suite as large as most houses. These were high rollers and Harry knew they expected the finest accommodations. Melanie conducted a tour for each guest. "This room has been electronically swept, so you'll have complete privacy. Your personal guards have access to our security if there are any questions or concerns. A specially appointed concierge will attend to all other matters."

"Got to admit, Harry Philer never disappoints."

"Anything else?"

"What time's the game tonight?"

"9:00 sharp."

The casino floor was dizzy with guests pushing slot machine buttons than rang, whistled, beeped and played catchy tunes. Colorful lasers flashed between the aisles while beautiful young ladies served cocktails on trays. Security was always present and cameras focused on every square inch of the casino. It was only on the third floor where the high rollers had private rooms. One such room had a plush white carpet with red trimmed borders and a green felt table gaming table. There was a stocked bar with expensive liquor and high priced modern furniture.

Harry and Melanie escorted the six players into the room where they had previously agreed to be accompanied by only one of their guards. The green table was stacked with cards and chips and their favorite alcoholic beverages were lined at the bar. Melanie strutted past them, drawing their lascivious eyes towards her. "Gentlemen, this room is completely private. You each have a phone under the table if anyone has a request."

Harry patted one of them on the shoulder. "Okay, guys. Have a great poker game. And may the best man win."

They left the room and one of them grabbed a deck of cards, shuffled and dealt out the first hand. "Five card draw. One thousand dollar ante."

"Oscar, how's your mama's feet?"

"They stink."

"Can't they do anything about it? Between your

farting and your mama, it must be real pleasant over at your place."

"It's a veritable flower shop."

"Edgar, what you did to Jimmy Caluzzi was a real piece of work."

He peeked at his cards. "I'll take two. Yeah, you guys always complained about him. But I took care of business."

"I hear you removed everything from his upper lip, down."

"Yeah, his tongue made a beautiful neck tie."

"I'll take three."

"Jimmy's dad had it better than him. At least they took his whole head."

"Fitting for a blabber mouth."

"I never got credit for mutilating Tommy Bolova."

"Karl, you messed up so many people we can't keep up. Still you took Bolova's left and right arm. I can't say he didn't deserve it."

"The man could never walk a straight line again, but boy he could move around them corners."

"I heard his whole family got whacked, kids too."

"I didn't do that. Let's face it, the guy pissed off a lot of people."

"But you did shoot off Benny's nose?"

"The sniffer?"

"All my work has a certain artistry to it."

Karl pushed his marker into the center of the table and showed three kings.

Oscar slammed his cards down on the table. "Damn!"

Edgar shook his head and folded. "And I had three of a kind."

"I'm out."

Karl swooped up the pile of chips. "It's all in the strategy, boys."

Another hand was dealt to everyone. "Say, anyone know anything about the Nansford killings?"

"They never found the old man's body parts."

"Two cards."

How about the chiseler, Larry Simms?"

"There's somebody nobody will miss."

"But cramming his eyeballs up his wazoo?"

"At least you'll always know where you're sitting. One card. Things is really changing. The old territories are disappearing."

"Four aces!"

"Anything on Arny the tub? I hear he went fishing in Australia. Somebody said his own lieutenants threw him overboard."

"Yeah, they landed a fifteen footer with him."

Karl tossed his cards down. "I'm out. When I whacked my uncle Fred, his birthday cake blew up in his face."

"You got style. I hear you dangled a guy off a fifty story building."

"Told me everything I wanted to know. If that pigeon wouldn't have shit on me, I might have held on better."

"Read um and weep. A full house."

"Anybody hear anything about the doctor?"

"He was the best plastic surgeon. I'd like to know who got him."

"I'm sure it was none of us. He was always useful."

"I hear it was just a dame cheating on her husband."

"The price of doing business out west."

"I've diversified. The feds are losing their grip. Problem is, things aren't doing much better in the rest of the world."

"Three cards."

"I'll take two. And go easy on me for a change."

Melanie strolled into Harry's office with a hand held computer. He was on a video phone, but ended his transmission. He grabbed a handful of peanuts and sipped up the last of his ice and whiskey. "Come in. I wanted to talk about Senator Darby's grandsons wedding."

"The arrangements have already been made."

"This is big, Blake. Darby has some influential friends in Washington."

"Since when are you interested in Washington politics?"

"Connections are always a good thing. Darby has power. He's a big player."

Melanie yawned. "These kinds of contacts haven't worked out in the past."

"Maybe so, but Darby's different. A senior senator."

"Don't worry, Harry. He'll be looked after properly."

He chewed his peanuts disgustingly. "I want the works. Spare no expense."

"The wedding's in the main ballroom. It took some doing, but we've hired a renowned ice sculpturist."

He sat back in his chair, impressed. "Ice in the desert. How good is that?"

"The fruit will be fresh, the food exquisite and the entertainment flawless. And you're set to give a short speech."

"Life is always good at the Extravaganza."

The senator's entourage arrived by helicopter and was ushered to an entire floor of penthouses. He was in the best of moods, tipping every employee and shaking hands with several guests. His wife was jolly, splashing her wine glass as she moseyed through the crowds. The bride's parents were beaming, proud to have their daughter marry into a prominent family. The groom was sent off to his bachelor party and the bride to her fitting room along with her giggly girlfriends.

The casino was like a termite's nest as gamblers played card games and fed slot machines. An occasional outburst from a winner interrupted the endless sounds coming from the machines. Encircling the casino floor were restaurants, cafes, expensive retail stores and the entrance to the main theatre. Harry was known to book first class talent and hired an international singing star for the wedding. "What do you think, Senator?"

Darby reclined in the chair across Harry's desk. "I'm impressed, Philer. You run a first class operation."

"We're here to please."

"Many of my colleagues and friends are curious about your little oasis out here. We're all anxious to do business with you."

"That's what I want to hear. There's no reason your friends in Washington should stay away." He opened a gold box on his desk. "Cuban?"

Harry flicked his platinum lighter as Darby puffed on the cigar. "Your security is quite impressive. I'm told you could survive a war."

"Your information is correct. Hopefully it won't come down to that."

"My friends and I are looking to expand our operations. Just because certain states have left the country doesn't mean we can't do business with them."

"Of course. I understand."

"California's a basket case, but Nevada is a different story."

"Las Vegas is a different story too, Senator. I'd stay away from there."

"Vegas is a shit hole. We're not interested in that. What we're looking for is a refuge of sorts."

Harry nodded confidently. "We honor privacy."

He puffed out a cloud of smoke. "I don't have to tell you things are getting pretty dangerous out there. A lot of people don't know this, but there was a small nuclear exchange in Pakistan a while back. It's only the first of what may be coming later. The Russians responded brutally. They clamped down on it for now."

"I had no idea."

"The Chinese have their own plans and Washington is still relatively safe. But that all could all change. That's where you come in."

"I'm sure we can come to a mutual understanding. If things get too nasty, you're always welcome here."

He tapped an ash into a tray. ""Thank's Philer. So let's get on with the festivities. I have a grandson to marry off."

July 2020

LES PALMER SHOVED HIS BLACK rimmed eyeglasses up the bridge of his nose and intensely studied a three dimensional computer schematic. He was employed by the FBI as an expert in micro-electronic surveillance technology. He toiled many hours at the J. Edgar Hoover building; preferring to work alone. He was thirty-two years old, thin but not gaunt and had an average appearance. Although his job did not entail the monitoring of cyberspace, he had developed many of those systems. He never created a weapon, but his parts were often used in the design.

A stout bald man, whose hairline shined in the fluorescent lights, barged into his lab with a coffee stained mug. "Time for a break, Les."

"That's easy for you to say. You're not behind."

He yawned. "You got to learn to relax."

"Like that's possible."

"You can find time to relax when you go to Colorado."

Irritated, Les squinted. "Oh, that's right. The annual technology show."

"The boss wants you there."

"Why? Every year I attend and there's nothing we haven't already invented. We're years ahead of the game."

"That's not the point. The President wants to know what's out there." He wiggled his eyebrows. "Besides, you get to party. Meet some girls."

He closed his eyes. "Yeah, I got that to look forward to."

"Cheer up, Les. It only gets better. Do you remember that briefing we have in fifteen minutes?"

He slapped both palms on his desk with a thud. "The stupid briefing!"

"I told you. It only gets better."

Palmer joined a group of badge wearing flunkies down the hallway towards a conference room. They all nudged through a door and took seats around a rectangular table. An elderly woman in a blue suit wandered up to the head of the table and opened her briefcase. "Good morning ladies and gentlemen. There have been many rumors about an incident that occurred a few months ago concerning a nuclear exchange in Pakistan. I can brief you on a few details, none of which are considered top secret. Still I suggest you keep this information within this room. Terrorists did manage to assemble a crude device and detonate it. The yield was low, and did cause some death and a certain amount of destruction. The Russians handled it in their usual way, and suffice it to say the families of those terrorists no longer exist. As far as the United States government is concerned, the case has been closed. However, our President still remains vigilant in protecting our citizens."

"So the Russians are cooperating?"

"In this matter, it appears so." There was muted laughter around the table. "We have updated some of the scenarios to deal with upcoming contingencies. These do not directly concern any of you, but that could always change. This concludes our meeting. You may resume your regular duties."

Les Palmer and a security guard boarded an Air

Force jet destined for Colorado. They flew at thirty thousand feet and circled the Rockies until landing at a small military base. They were driven by car to a hotel near the conference center where technology firms from all over the globe would display their newest gadgets. They checked into their rooms, had dinner and retired early that evening.

The following day Les sauntered past sales booths containing products that his division had developed years earlier. As with every year he attended, Les was bored with the inferior surveillance equipment and facial identification software. He nodded impatiently while each dealer bragged about their state of the art technology.

Palmer's security guard remained at a distance from him as he reluctantly surveyed the wares. Les was ready to go back to his hotel room when he gazed across the room and thought he recognized a woman staring at him. He stopped, focused in on her and then excused himself while dissecting his way through the crowds. When he got close, he knew exactly who it was. "Melanie Blake? What are you doing here?"

"Hello, Les. Surprised to see me?" She peered over his shoulder at his security guard. "That your man?"

"Yeah, my security." He shook his head. "And to answer your question, yes, I'm quite surprised." He waved off the guard. "It's been, what, five years?"

"Four and a half, but who's counting. I came here hoping to see you."

"I thought we were over."

She hugged him timidly. "You broke up with me if I remember correctly."

He pushed her away gently. "Really? I recall you wanted to move to Nevada to work for Harry Philer. You gave up on me."

"It was an opportunity of a lifetime."

He frowned. "To work for a crook?"

"And who's honest these days?"

His grinned with familiarity. "Here we go again. The same old arguments."

She held his hand. "You're right. I'm not here to fight ghosts."

"So why are you here?"

"To see you."

"Okay, I'm here."

"Have dinner with me tonight? Just the two of us."

He hesitated, and then nodded. "Sure, why not."

"I'll make the reservations."

Les resumed his foray along the convention floor, finally calling it quits when he was satisfied that the government was not threatened by any new technology. He went back to his room, told the guard he was having dinner alone and freshened up before meeting Melanie at an expensive steak house.

He arrived on time to find her smartly attired in a white dress and gold hoped earrings. The hostess brought them over to a secluded candle lit table with propped up napkins and shiny silverware. Melanie ordered a gin martini and he a scotch on the rocks.

"So, here we are."

Les draped the napkin over his lap. "Yes, we are. So you wanted to talk?"

She tilted her martini glass. "To the point, Les. I

like that. Before I tell you, I just wanted you to know that I really did love you. It may interest you to know that there's been no one else."

His eyes widened. "Really?"

"How about you? I know a few ladies that were interested."

He glanced away shyly. "Well…nothing worked out."

"I'm surprised."

"Really? Because you're hot. You can get any guy you want."

"I'm flattered. But that's not exactly true."

He tapped the table. "I got to ask you, Melanie. Why Harry Philer over the Bureau?"

"Serving my country, you mean? I remember many a conversation where you were fed up with how things were going."

"Fed up, but not ready to quit." He cleared his throat. "So why are we here?"

She squeezed his hand. "I know you disapprove of Harry. But my loyalty only goes so far. What I'm about to tell you has nothing to do with Harry Philer or his interests. It's quite the opposite."

He pulled away. "So let's hear it."

"What do you know about the Abel Crawley film?"

"The UFO thing? Don't you guys show it at the Extravaganza?"

"Harry charges a pretty penny for viewing it."

He snickered. "It's a fake."

She sipped her martini. "Are you sure of that?"

"You're going to tell me it's real?"

She paused and poked her cheek out with her tongue. "It is real."

He gulped the rest of his scotch. "Yeah, right. Come on, what's this really about?"

"I've seen it many times. Believe me, it looks real to me."

"And so were the alien autopsies. This is ridiculous, Melanie. What proof do you have that it's real?"

"To be honest with you; I never gave the film much thought until David Logan paid me a visit."

"David came to the hotel?"

"You wouldn't think this was the kind of place he would visit."

"What does the Crawley film have to do with David Logan?"

"He was convinced it was real. Your mentor and my friend believed the Crawley film was absolutely authentic. Did you know he was the first to analyze it at the Bureau? He was working on a program similar to Project Blue Book. He came to Extravaganza to view the film one last time. Six months later he died of cancer. He left me with some interesting artifacts. And that's where you come in."

"Logan was a skeptic. He never believed in flying saucers."

The waiter came to take their order. "We'll talk later. In the meantime, let's enjoy some really good porterhouses."

They finished dinner and ordered a bottle of port wine. Still engaged in light conversation, Les was bothered by David's professed belief in the UFO film. When they drank the last of the port, Melanie convinced him to come up to her room. He was reluctant, and yet his curiosity overwhelmed any doubts. She swiped her hotel room card, went over to the curtains and opened them to reveal the clear Colorado night. "Les, how much do you know about Abel Crawley?"

"Nothing."

"Abel Crawley was not just some kook. He was a physicist at Cal-Tech. He was a believer in extraterrestrial life. But he wasn't a fanatic by any stretch of the imagination. The story goes he shot this eight millimeter film in 1968 on a farm, or a ranch, or something in-between; capturing a flying saucer. He first showed the film to a childhood friend named Tim Harter; a plumber of all things living in Stockton, California. He tells Harter that the saucer often visits this farm and it was a way to leave the planet if one desired. Of course Harter thinks his friend's a little crazy, but doesn't think much else after that. And then in 1969 Crawley tells Harter that he thinks his wife and nine year old son are imposters."

"What do you mean?"

"He tells Harter they are duplicates. Of course Harter now thinks his friend has gone over the deep end. So Crawley visits Harter one last time and gives him the UFO film and several other reels of family footage. He walks out the door and nobody ever sees him again. Harter turns the films over to the government and that's when David Logan gets his first look."

"He authenticated it?"

"He was originally brought on to debunk flying saucer stuff. As far as the government was concerned, it had to be a fake. And David set out to convince the government it was a fake."

Les seemed irritated. "David never talked about it to me. But to you, he talked about everything. That's how it always was; he always confided in you. Pissed me off. He always felt more comfortable talking to you."

"David used the best equipment he had at the time; dissecting the film frame by frame. Of course Crawley hand held his camera and it is shaky. But the picture is really clear. Two known still pictures were released to the public which have been reproduced in many UFO books. But those were terrible copies and had been debunked as hoaxes. But the film footage was never released. David could never absolutely prove the contents of the film were authentic. But he was fairly certain that it was not tampered with in any way." She removed her shoes and tossed them in the corner of the room."

"Same old Melanie."

"So, I'm a slob. I'm sure you're still the clean freak."

"We haven't changed."

"David concluded there were three distinctive traits in the footage that gave it credibility. First, the actual saucer. In ninety percent, perhaps ninety-five percent of UFO footage the saucer is always moving behind objects such as trees, mountains and buildings. The saucer in the Crawley footage is in front of things. This gives us solid perspective; much more difficult to hoax. Secondly there's a farmer in the picture; an eyewitness other than the camera operator. And thirdly, and most astonishing, the saucer accelerates twenty feet or so at a tremendous speed. Though the film is shaky at times, Crawley's camera is not moving the scene along. David told me this kind of technology is not even possible today, let alone in 1968.

Les collapsed on the sofa and covered his face and moaned. "So you believe that Crawley actually filmed a UFO?"

"I do."

"How did Harry Philer get a hold of it?"

"That's a mystery. As far as David knew, the government never released the footage to the public and it was supposedly just stored in a basement with little or no security. Whether or not the film was authentic, David believed the government was not interested in finding out the truth. When the freedom of information act came out, Harter was already dead and his family asked for the film. Somehow it was never located. And then Harry Philer gets a hold of it. I only know he paid well for it. But he's never told me the origin of the acquisition. And David told me there were no copies."

"This all seems so wierd."

She paced the floor. "The mystery of how Harry got the film has no bearing. All I care about is the film."

"And you really believe Harry's got the only copy?"

"Yep. And it's protected by a security system as advanced as anything out there."

"I still can't get over the fact that David Logan thought it was real."

"Unfortunately he was never able to find the farm.

He was too sick in the end to even try. But he did manage to get a hold of some additional material; including the Crawley home films. They were going to throw them away. He kept them all this time."

"All right, assuming the film is real, and I have my doubts about that, what do you propose to do about it?"

She angled behind the sofa and tenderly cradled his shoulders. "David insisted that by finding the farm, one could escape the earth. And that's what I want to do. Get off before it's too late."

He turned around with a shocked expression. "Are you kidding me?"

"David could never find the clue that would lead to the farm's location. But he tried. The only real hint is a faded sign on the barn with what appears to be the letters, 'LER'. The 'L' is barely legible."

"So we're looking for the Maller, Caller, Baller farm? There are probably a million possibilities."

"Maybe ten million."

He stood up. "So where do I come in?"

She sucked in a deep breath. "You possess the technology to make a copy of the film. And not only that, the scanning equipment you have today far exceeds that of what David had to work with. I want to find that farm, Les."

"So you can meet a few Martians?"

"Les, how much longer do you think this world of ours has? Do you seriously believe we're heading for a new peace and prosperity? I don't think so. Things are bad, and getting worse."

"I'll admit things don't look promising right now."

"I like the odds off the planet."

"Melanie, this is crazy. How are we going to steal the film?"

She pointed her finger high in the air. "Glad you asked. I'm in charge of security, so leave that part up to me. You have a different job. When I was at the Bureau, you were developing a new kind of eye lens camera."

"It's done. Fits over the cornea and is virtually undetectable. But it's not invulnerable to an advanced electronic scanning system like you have at the hotel. But I have a feeling you can compensate for that."

"They'll be a minor split second power fluctuation."

"Won't they become suspicious?"

"It won't be significant enough to draw attention. Besides, I'll cover you."

"Looks like you thought of everything."

"By the time they figure it out, we'll be long gone."

"Philer's going to know it was an expert job."

"He will. But he won't find out for a long time."

He walked over to her. "So you really want to do this?"

"You must have a lot of accumulated leave? If it's the same old Les, you probably have a wealth of stored hours?"

"They're begging me to take off. You want to know the truth, I'm not really that important to them any longer. New breeds of young scientists are producing more for them every day."

"I run the security checks on all our guests. I'll give you a false identity."

He placed his fingers on each side of his temples. "I got to think about it, Melanie. This is all too much. I mean, you hurt me once before."

"I chose a career over you, and I'm sorry about that. But this is really big." She opened one of her suitcases and removed a small box. "These are Abel Crawley's home films. Eight millimeter rolls. Take them and analyze them. See if Crawley was right about his wife and kid."

He held up one roll of film. "If there's nothing here, I'm not inclined to go through with this."

"Fair enough." She wandered over to him, threw her arms over his shoulders and kissed him sensuously."

"What was that for?"

"Les, I missed you so much. I never really loved anyone else." She unbuttoned his shirt. "I want you tonight."

He leaned in and kissed her on the neck and rubbed her arms. "Are you sure?"

"More than ever."

He slid his arm down to her waist, took her by the other hand and brought her into the bedroom where they feverishly undressed each other. They wrapped the bed sheets around their naked bodies and their hands glided over sensuous mounds of quivering flesh. She screamed with joy, secretly regretting those years of absence from him. He too realized that she was always the right one for him. They made love all night as if it would not happen again.

Les arrived back in Washington in a much better mood than when he had left. He sent a report to his boss that indicated the government's edge in technology was secured and then worked on some unfinished projects. Once completed, he removed the Crawley home films from the box and scanned them onto a computer in his laboratory. He had the ability to not only view the footage, but analyze it with infrared, spectral and quality enhancement programs.

The first reel was labeled January of 1967. He ran the footage at normal speed, revealing a picnic setting where a woman, apparently Abel Crawley's wife, sat relaxed with friends at a table in a public park. She was wearing a blue patterned shirt and white pants and had a white scarf around her neck. Soon a young boy skipped up to her, faced the camera and waved. They both smiled and waved at the camera and another male adult came over to them. The woman stood up and they all smiled and waved at the camera. The remainder of the footage was of a picnic lunch and typical park games such as horseshoes and croquet.

Les viewed another reel labeled November of 1968. It was similar to the 1967 film in that it was another outdoor setting; a Halloween pumpkin patch with straw wagons and paper machete witches. This film particularly intrigued Les because there were many full body shots of the same woman wearing a red checkered blouse and dress, watching her son feed some goats and pigs. As in the previous reel, mother and son stood in front of the camera and waved to who was presumably Abel Crawley. The boy ran over, picked up a small pumpkin and handed it to his mother. The film ended as they waved and mouthed words to the camera.

The next film was titled February of 1969. The film was taken at yet another outdoor location; a lake with pine trees near a shoreline. There were a group of adults and children next to trailers near a camp site. Mrs. Crawley appeared again, this time wearing a green blouse with blue pants. She stood in the center of the film and waved over her young son, who brought a small trout hanging on the end of a fishing line. The final footage was labeled March of 1969 when mother and son were alone in their backyard next to a table and swing set. Mrs. Crawley was in green and yellow polka dot dress and their son was dressed in a cowboy outfit. They paraded in front of the camera, sometimes stopping to wave. Les watched the remainder of the film, which mostly had Mrs. Crawley pushing her son on the swing set.

"That's it", he muttered. "Now to the hard work."

He reviewed the original 1967 film and isolated several frames of Mrs. Crawley in her blue shirt and white pants. From there he took comparative dimensions of her with microscopic accuracy and then did the same for her son. Following that procedure, he now had the exact height and weight of both of them. He zoomed in on their faces and repeated the accurate tracing of the various features and skin tones. When it was all completed, he fed the information into the computer and produced three dimensional diagrams of their body and faces. He followed the same procedure with the other three films and now had the ability for detailed comparison.

"Now to crunch the numbers."

Within two hours, he had all the information he needed. He examined it thoroughly, pushed himself away from the desk and dropped his jaw in amazement.

"Son of a bitch."

August 2020

MELANIE BLAKE WAS WORKING IN her office at 10:00 in the evening when her phone rang. She picked it up and Les was on the other line. "Is this secure?"

She punched in a few buttons. "Les, it's safe to talk."

"My scans concur."

"I haven't heard from you in weeks. I was beginning to worry."

He hesitated. "Yeah, sorry about that. We had such a good time. I guess I got cold feet or something."

"What about the films?"

"That's why I'm calling you. I'm getting shudders down my body even talking about it. Abel Crawley was right."

"I knew it."

"Melanie, these are untouched films. No sign of doctoring. I've gone over and over it. The earliest films, the 1967 and 1968 footage are of the same woman and child. They had the same body mass, the same facial discolorations, bumps and blotches. But the later films weren't the same people. Close…but not the same. They are almost perfect, but there are enough differences to discount a perfect match. Keep in mind, to the naked eye you couldn't tell. But the computer program is conclusive. The original Mrs. Crawley had a mild browning spot on her forehead.

You could hardly see it, but the 1969 Mrs. Crawley had no such blotching. And the tracing didn't match. Their body measurements were different. Very slight height and weight differences. But enough to verify that Abel Crawley was not out of his mind. He was right. These were not members of his family."

"That's why David saved the films."

"He must have known for sure. So now we're left with something we don't have an explanation for."

"Les, we got to find out."

He inhaled at what seemed to be an eternity. "Okay, you win. There's enough evidence to take a good look at this film of yours."

"I'll make the arrangements."

"I'll be using a special dampening filed to conceal my luggage contents at the airports and at your hotel. But once I'm in, it's up to you."

Les entered his superior's office. "Palmer, you wanted to see me?"

"Yes sir. I need to take a week off."

He looked up, startled. "You?"

"Yes sir. My sister's in Florida. I need to visit her."

He smiled. "Great. That's great. Take two weeks."

"One will be enough. Are you sure you can spare me?"

"If you don't take some of that time, you're going to lose it. Go see your family. You deserve it."

"Thank you, sir. I appreciate it."

Les packed his suitcase and boarded a plane to Las Vegas. Waiting there was a van from the Extravaganza which took him and four other guests to the hotel. When they arrived, Melanie greeted them, hardly acknowledging Les as planned. She escorted them to the VIP registration where the luggage was brought to their rooms. Les held his attaché case close to his side as he swiped his room card in the door. He was checked into a moderate suite that had such amenities as freshly cut flowers, a fruit basket, a bottle of wine and a small box of candies.

He noticed a blinking light on the phone. He picked it up and listened to a short message until a real person came on the line. "Welcome Mr. Jestin, this is the concierge desk. We've extended you a gambling credit and want to know what events you're interested in. May we suggest the UFO excursion?"

"No, but I want to see the Crawley film."

"We have a show available tonight at 11:30 at the UFO theatre. Your ticket will be available at the box office."

"That's fine. I'll be there."

He set his attaché case down on the desk, showered under four gushing spigots and dressed in a casual sports coat and ate dinner at an Italian restaurant. He had complimentary tickets to a musical act of which he knew nothing of; and afterwards played slot machines for an hour. By 10:00 in the evening he had enough of the casino noise and went back up to his room.

Les disengaged the dampening field on his attaché case, opened it up and revealed two small black cases and some wrapped wires. In one case there was a three inch by half inch rectangular device that powered the camera system. In the other were the two contact lenses that would record the film. He dropped the power unit into an interior coat pocket and took the contacts into the bathroom where he spread out a gelatinous substance and eyewash near the sink. He carefully placed a lens onto his right eye, then his left. For the next half an hour he practiced walking around the room to adapt to the slightly obscured vision.

Les nervously exited his room and rode the elevator to the theater on the mezzanine level. He picked up his ticket and waited in line with the other guests eager to see the show. Melanie stood in front a power console in the security section where she was a normal visitor. While the employees monitored activities at their panels, she discreetly entered a code that would momentarily disrupt the power to the theater doorway.

Melanie peered at her watch, pushed a button and a silent alarm indicated a power fluctuation. She turned to her nearest employee. "What just happened?"

"I don't know, Miss Blake. An interruption."

She looked over her power station controls. "Yeah, I see it. What do you think could have caused it?"

"I'm not sure. But it didn't seem to affect any systems."

"Run a diagnostic. I don't see any damage on any pivotal systems. If you don't find anything, we'll just consider it an anomaly and file a report.

Les sat comfortably in one of the velvet rocking chairs and waited for all the chattering guests to find their seats. Eventually the lights dimmed, the voices quieted and the screen revealed Harry Philer pompously seated behind his desk. "Welcome ladies and gentlemen to the wonderful Extravaganza hotel and casino. You are about to watch a rare piece of film shot by Cal-Tech physicist, Abel Crawley in 1968. Mr. Crawley never identified the location of the event. All I can say is that it is the best evidence of extraterrestrial life ever recorded. You can make your own judgments about its authenticity. To date, no official government agency has been able to prove it false. We will show the film twice; first in slow motion, and then at normal speed. Before we do that, please enjoy this twenty minute history of unidentified flying objects throughout the ages."

Les impatiently viewed former well known UFO images he had seen before. The lights eventually dimmed for the Crawley footage. With the tap of a button inside his coat, he activated the eye cameras and began to record the film. Grabbing onto the chair arms tightly, he kept his head as steady as possible. The eight millimeter color film started in slow motion as a shaky hand revealed an open yard extending up to a large tree next to a few smaller eucalyptus trees. And then a silverfish blue saucer like craft appeared in the frame in front of the large tree. Although it didn't display the usual saucer rotation, it slowly moved in front of the eucalyptus trees and then suddenly sped up to what appeared to be fast motion for about twenty feet until it slowed down again. At that moment, Crawley swung the camera over to a big headed farmer in overalls next to a barn door. The farmer, who had a long protruding chin, pointed at the saucer which now arrived in the view of the camera just over the barn roof. This is where the letters, 'LER' appeared high over the barn door. The farmer kept pointing at the saucer, which lifted above the barn roof and out of sight. The film ended.

Mesmerized, the guests began to clap and mutter

to each other. Soon the film began at regular speed where the twenty foot spurt from the saucer seemed incredibly fast. At that time Melanie was at another power console with her eyes fixed on her watch. She inconspicuously entered a code and waited. Les had turned off the camera device and strolled out of the theater. Melanie had disengaged the power once again and another technician notified her. She repeated her instructions to run a diagnostic.

Les packed his suitcase, got undressed and went to bed. Flushed with adrenaline and eyes wide open, it took three hours before he could actually go to sleep. Two mornings' later he was driven in the company van to Las Vegas and boarded a plane for Washington. He wanted so much to get back to work and analyze the film, but had to sit home for a few days because his boss still thought he was in Florida. Those days were agonizingly long and all he could do was sit in front of the television.

Harry was in his office watching the news when Melanie entered. He ignored her, transfixed by events. "Can you believe this shit?"

"What's going on?"

"Russia's moving into Poland. What is this, the 1940's? That means they have the territory back when they were Soviets."

"I hear they may make a move for Germany."

"We won't do anything to stop them, that's for sure."

She snickered. "Harry, are you saying it's an unpredictable world?"

"Your damn right it is. That's why it's everybody for themselves."

"War used to be good business. I'm not so sure anymore."

Harry scratched his crotch boldly. "I hear we had a couple of power failures yesterday."

"I wouldn't call them failures, but we did have unexplained fluctuations."

"Has that ever happened before?"

"It happens a few times a year. It's usually nothing. But I'm running diagnostics."

"Well, keep on it."

"Harry, everything's fine."

"That's what I want to hear. But keep checking into it. It makes me uneasy. Double, triple check it if you have to."

"I'm on it." She began to walk out of the office. "Is there anything else?"

His eyes turned back to the news. "Nahh, just world crap."

Les Palmer had become claustrophobic in his apartment by the time he went back to work. He was asked to decipher a code for Special Forces operations in South Dakota, which only took him a few hours. He was just about to proceed with the Crawley film when another department head rushed in with another electronic problem. He adjusted his equipment and promised results in two hours, but finished in less than an hour. Lunch time came around and he sat in the cafeteria with several colleagues. When he got back to his laboratory he finally had freedom to download the film on his elaborate computer program.

Les removed the recording device from his attaché and took out a wafer thin chip. He placed it on a special duplication unit and transferred it to his computer. After carefully layering the original footage on multiple film surfaces, he downloaded the master software into his personal lap top computer and made one copy for reserve. He then removed all traces of his work and left the Bureau for home.

It was midnight at the Extravaganza and the casino was a cacophony of loud music, theatrical shows, the desert UFO tours and the regular showings of the Crawley film. Harry was sleeping soundly in his penthouse when he was alerted by security. He quickly changed into his clothes, rode his private elevator down the basement and was greeted by a nervous guard. "What's this all about?"

"My name is Carlson, sir. I'm sorry to wake you."

"Why didn't you call Blake?"

"She didn't respond."

"What's the problem?"

His voice cracked. "I was at a power panel the other night when we had those interruptions. I don't think it was a failure."

His face turned fierce. "What?"

"Melanie Blake was a few feet away. She ordered me to run diagnostics. I didn't find any cause of power drains, fluctuations or relay failures. I think Miss Blake caused them deliberately."

"What proof do you have?"

"Nothing seemed to comprehend. And then I remembered she was at the console. I ran a diagnostic. It was there all right. There was direct interference. The modulator was rerouted. Only one reason to do that. Make it look like an anomaly."

"But why would she do that?" He jolted, snapping his fingers. "Shit, the Crawley film!"

"What do you mean, sir?"

"What time was the first failure?"

"It must have been around 11:15."

"And there was a show at eleven thirty." He slammed his fist on a console top. "I'm in deep shit." He called in his second in command, who had been off duty for a few hours. "Find Blake and get her in here."

"Yes, Mr. Philer."

Harry retreated to his office and paced like a father waiting for a child to be born. The second in command came into the office. "Well...?"

"I'm sorry, Mr. Philer. She's no where to be found."

"Damn it, she's long gone by now."

Les Palmer had worked another full day in his laboratory, finishing up on a new electronic jamming device. Although he was not the designer of the equipment, his expertise was always appreciated by the younger scientists. He packed up his attaché case, said goodbye to his colleagues and drove home. He parked his car, hiked up the ten steps to his apartment building, checked his mailbox and walked towards his unit at the end of the hallway. About to turn his key in the door, a silent alarm in his cell phone vibrated in his pocket.

Frozen, he shook his head, removed a small pistol from his pocket and scurried out of the building and into his car. He opened his lap top, punched in a few codes and activated a hidden light sensitive camera inside his unit. He scanned the room and to his surprise, Melanie Blake was seated in one of his leather chairs. He closed his lap top, ran back up the stairs, opened the door and turned on the lights.

"What the hell's going on here?"

She stood up, embraced him and kissed him on the lips. "So you have your own personal security system?"

"Melanie, what are you doing here?"

"Plans have changed. I've been made."

"I thought you said he wouldn't find out."

"I was wrong. I had to run. And there's another problem. He's going to find out it was you."

"Please tell me that's not true."

"Sorry, Les. Harry's got a friend in congress. He'll get a make on you."

Les kicked the bottom of the chair. "That's great. That's just great."

"There's nothing I can do. You're in."

"I can come clean at the Bureau."

"Do you think they'll be helpful?"

"No. I'm screwed."

"You got to trust me, Les. I know what I'm doing."

"Sure you do. What's next?"

"We need two sets of false identifications." She reached into her purse and pulled out a small disc. "My photo and info. Can you do it?"

"That's easy", he uttered exasperatedly. "They'll never know it came from their own system."

"Make us agricultural agents; considering we're looking for a farm. And then we need two licenses with an Illinois address for Alison and James Dunston. It's all on the disc."

"I can do all that."

"Wish we could leave tonight."

"I'll go to work tomorrow, get the ID's and put in for a two week leave. This has to be done right."

"I understand. Now you know what you're doing."

His worried expression turned to enthusiasm. "Melanie, I've scanned the Crawley film for tampering. It's original footage. No insertions. It's fantastic."

"Awesome. That's what I wanted to here."

He grabbed onto her arms. "My equipment can detect alterations even from the most modern special effects. But back in 1968, special effects were in their infant stages. I scanned the blank sections of the film; you know the areas between tree leaves. There's no wires, no insertions. The film's clean. Whatever this vehicle is; it's really there. Not a fake. It could be a balloon, but it's really there."

"It's extraterrestrial."

"I'm not going that far. The only thing I know is I can't explain it. The way the saucer speeds up is remarkable."

"We got to find this farm."

He nodded. "I think so. This technology is beyond us."

"Then you're on board?"

"What choice do I have? You've made it already."

Harry's new head of security brought in a photograph of Les palmer entering the theater. "We've run a check on everybody, and this person does not exist."

Harry grunted, and then swallowed a handful

of peanuts. "Melanie's plant. She gave him a false name."

"That's confirmed. She personally admitted him."

"Damn, they got my film."

"Mr. Philer, we have no idea of this man's identity."

"I think I know. Or at least who he works for. He's got to be one of Blake's former FBI friends. And somebody with access to some pretty sophisticated technology."

"What are we going to do?"

"You're excused." Harry watched him leave the room and then made a phone call. "Senator Darby, this is Harry Philer. I hope this is a secure line?"

"Sure is, Harry. What can I do for you?"

"I'm going to email you a photograph of a man. I think he works for the FBI. I need an identification."

"My pleasure. We're still talking about that great wedding."

"This has to be discreet. I don't want the individual or his bosses to know about the inquiry."

"I have direct access on my committee. Consider it done."

"Thanks' Senator. I owe you." Harry hung up and immediately made another call. "Hello, Karl. It's Philer. I'm going to need a favor in the Washington DC area. I need you to fix something."

"What's going on?"

"Melanie Blake, a former employee. She stole something from me. The Crawley film; or at least a copy of it. I'm going to need information on its whereabouts, so use drugs. Once that's done, you can torture her. As matter of fact, take a little bit off her every day for all I care."

Les and Melanie made love that evening, rekindling their romance. She rested against his chest and stroked his hair and forehead. Although he was still suspicious of her motives, he couldn't help but to love the woman he had once lost. They slept contently until the morning hours when Les had to leave. Once at the Bureau, he prepared and laminated the two sets of identification. He was especially proud of the quality of the FDA badges that had the names of Charles Dartell and Kristin Mathers.

Les contacted his boss in the afternoon hours and requested a meeting. Nervous, he entered the office, waited about twenty minutes and finally sat down across from him. "So Palmer, what can I do for you?"

"I know I just took a vacation, but I need to take a little more time."

"Oh...?"

"Two more weeks."

"Use or lose it, I always say. We can do with out you here for a while."

"I appreciate that. I've caught up on all my projects."

"That was never in question. You take care of yourself."

Les packed up and walked out of the Bureau at 7:30 that evening. Just as a precautionary matter he opened his lap top in his car and scanned the apartment before entering. He was stunned to see Melanie holding a gun on four men who were tied up and gagged on the couch and chairs. He quickly jolted up the stairs and into his apartment. "What the hell's going on?"

"Harry found us."

"Who are these people?"

"Mob friends. He found out who you were and where you lived. The boss is Karl Benson. One mean son of a bitch. But I was waiting for them."

"What?"

She pulled him into the bedroom and whispered to him. "You don't understand. We've been made. You can't ever go back to work. We got to hit the road."

"What!"

"Harry's apparently has good FBI contacts, and we know his friends are organized crime. He won't stop until he kills us both."

"I didn't sign up for this."

"You're in it, whether you like it or not. From now on we can't trust anybody."

"What about these guys?"

She cocked her head and stared compassionately. "I know you won't let me kill them. Fortunately we don't have to. They won't be able to track us. I'm really good at this kind of thing."

"What about the Bureau?"

"I guarantee you that Harry isn't going share info with the FBI. And the Bureau has no love lost for him either." She kissed his cheek. "We're already packed and ready to go."

"Where?"

"Pennsylvania. We'll park your car and rent a vehicle there. Our destination is California. I trust you have the film and the ID's?"

"All with me."

"Then what are we waiting for."

Les drove them out of Washington and through dark stretches of Virginia roads occasionally interrupted by small towns. They headed north to Pennsylvania, where Les asked if it was safe to travel on the interstate. Melanie assured him that Karl could not track them. After a few hours they arrived in New Castle, Pennsylvania and turned into a car rental lot. "Les, I'm going to use my real name for a two week rental."

"Is that wise?"

"Better me than you. Harry's looking for me, but the Bureau has more tentacles, if you know what I mean. Not that they'll be looking for you right away. Besides, this should be our last rental. If all goes well, we'll find the farm."

"You're an optimist, Melanie. But like you said, we can't go back now."

"We'll ditch your car in a mall somewhere."

Melanie emerged from the rental office with a packet and keys. Les joined her and they located their designated mid sized white sedan. Melanie started the car and rolled out onto Highway 80 in a westerly direction. Although it was late night, there was a steady stream of oncoming headlights all the way to the Ohio border. Melanie eventually spotted a motel with a vacancy sign in one of the sleepy towns off the highway. They registered under the name of James Dunston, Les's false identity and paid cash with a portion of the thirty thousand dollars Melanie had packed in her suitcase.

Exhausted, they checked into the room, fell face

forward on the bed and fell asleep without uttering a word. By mid morning the next day, Les was already seated at the desk studying his lap top when Melanie opened up her eyes. She groaned, tugged on the disheveled blankets and yawned loudly. "Morning."

"About time you got up."

"What are you up to?"

"Just looking at the program. I want to study this film. I'm going to look at this thing frame by frame."

"Sounds good. Hungry?"

"A little."

She yawned again. "I'm starved."

"Now that we've determined the footage is real, I'm taking a close look at the lettering. Although the 'L' is faint, it's definitely the letter 'L'. And for some reason, the paint on preceding letters is missing. Probably faded away."

"Any lingering paint chips?"

"I've scanned it on a molecular level. So far I've uncovered the remnants of another possible preceding letter."

She wandered up behind him. "Really?"

"Take a look. Maybe some paint chips. But they're dispersed. Worn away. Let me zoom as close as I can without losing contrast." He manipulated his computer keyboard. "Here we go. That's pretty good. There's the curved form of a letter. Extrapolating from this, it could be a 'D", a 'G', an 'O', 'Q', 'U', or possibly even an 'S'."

She cringed. "That doesn't narrow it down much."

"Judging by the size of the sign and its letters, there's probably only enough room for three more preceding letters. So we're looking at a six letter name. Unfortunately that's the best I can do. But at least we have something we didn't know before. David's technology could not have found this."

"So there's still a lot of possibilities; but we're closer."

"I've been studying the barn for the last hour and there appears to be no other markings or letters. It's just an old wooden barn. The wood is weathered, but there's nothing there to indicate any signs or words."

Melanie grabbed the top of her hair. "Oh, I must look a fright."

He wiggled his eyebrows. "I think you look pretty nice."

She hugged him. "I'll shower."

"I already have."

"After, we'll get something to eat."

"Don't get discouraged, Mel. We've just begun analyzing this thing. We'll come up with something tangible."

While Melanie showered, Les continued to scan the footage. She dried off, got dressed and they walked across the street to a diner with acceptably good coffee. They ordered bacon and eggs; hers over easy and his scrambled. The waitress brought the plates and Les smiled broadly. "Smells good."

"I'm hungry." Melanie picked up a piece of bacon and chewed heartily. "Wow, this is probably from a nearby farm."

"The Batler farm?"

"Funny. I can come up with names, too."

He gazed suspiciously at the other patrons, as well

as the cars zipping past the highway. "You don't think they can find us here?"

"Relax, Les. We'll be all right. It's a big country. Harry's connected, but the mob's not an organized police force. The world's going to hell in a hand basket and they have even less influence than before."

"Still, I'm worried."

She smiled, sopping up the egg yolk with her toast. "That's my baby. You do the worrying and I'll take care of business."

"What about Karl? We left him in my apartment."

"His friends have already freed them by now."

Les saw the waitress and raised his coffee cup above his head. "At least we're not a security risk."

"The Bureau won't be coming for us either. At least for now. Remember, you're on vacation."

"Just think, a couple of weeks ago I had a normal life. And now I'm like a fugitive. It's disconcerting, to say the least."

"But it's an adventure, huh?"

"Real adventure. Chasing a UFO."

Melanie finished eating her bacon. "David thought it was important."

"For all we know, Abel Crawley could have just gone off and committed suicide."

"Les, this earth of ours has its days numbered. After humans are gone, the crickets and birds can have it."

"We've been lucky so far that we haven't had any major nuclear or biological attacks. But you're right, Mel. That could change any time"

"Come on, we got to go."

"Where now?"

"Highway 80 all the way to Reno, and then California."

"Are you sure staying on the highways is a good idea?"

"We just have to keep clear of the more dangerous big cities. Places like Los Angeles and San Francisco."

Les drove the car through Ohio, Illinois and Iowa. They kept watching off the side of the road, hoping to see the farm. They knew their efforts were futile and the odds were infinitesimal that it would be situated near the highway. There were many towns, many billboards, water towers, windmills, some working and some decrepit; and the ubiquitous collection of barns and farm houses.

At twilight they stopped near the Iowa, Nebraska border and investigated a farm that had similarities to the one in the film. A sense of excitement filled them as they turned off the side of the road and surveyed the barn behind a low wooden fence. It was similar, but there were no trees or a sign above the barn. Without delay, they resumed their route down highway 80 through Nebraska. As night fell they turned off the highway near the town of North Plate and into a neon bathed motel parking lot half full of vehicles.

Les held up the ice bucket, pushed the button on the machine and waited impatiently for the ice to drop. After a few cubes hit the bucket he was satisfied with the meager amount. Melanie watched the television news coverage of the distress in Europe and Russia. Les poured two sodas, opened up his lap top and began to examine the Crawley footage. "Melanie, come over here and take a look at this."

"What do you got?"

"I'm zooming in on the big tree to the right of the screen. I got to think; maybe somebody carved their names on the bark. Lovers, kids, who knows."

She turned off the television. "Sounds reasonable."

"Could we be so lucky to find Bill loves Suzy?"

"How close can you get?"

"Check it out. That's a moth on the bark of that tree trunk."

"What kind of moth? That could narrow our search."

Les threw up his hands. "How the hell should I know? It looks like any moth."

"Still, it's a clue."

"We'd have to delve into the internet to find out."

"That wouldn't be wise right now. We have to stay invisible."

"I'm now going to scan for some kind of sign; something on a board, some kind of marker. Anything." He meticulously examined every frame near and behind the trees for a posted sign, stick or board. The resolution was clear, but they could not identify any lettering. He kept scanning up and down the tree trunks in hopes of finding carvings, but was unsuccessful.

"Les, this is a dead end."

"But it's worth going over. I've got a program that detects anomalies of any kind. Right now where looking for anything raised off a surface. If that doesn't work, we'll scan the frames with infrared."

"What about the saucer?"

"Let's take a detailed look."

"I'm for anything."

"Here it comes entering the frame right. I'll slow it down. Now let's examine the metallic surface. It's burnished, a little rough. Judging by the sunlight I'd say we're looking at mid afternoon. Here's the most amazing thing. The shadow. It doesn't stay in the frame long, but it correlates perfectly with the saucer. This thing is really in the sky. It still could be a balloon, or something else; but it's definitely not a special effect. Now the sudden burst of speed." He stopped the frame. "Here's where David was absolutely right. There is no earthly science or technology that can attain this speed." He resumed the footage. "I'm going to keep this real slow. Watch the sun reflection. It remains on the right section of the surface. Here it goes. And it's so fast that even in slow motion it blurs. And that blur is a direct result of the speed outpacing the camera. The integrity of the saucer remains in tact." He gazed at her, baffled. "This thing is real. We're looking at a vessel from another world. There can be no other conclusion."

"You're only verifying what I've known all along."

"This is big, Melanie. Abel Crawley might have been an eccentric, but he was not lying about his experience."

"So how fast do you think that thing was going?"

"I can only roughly calculate the speed burst is thirty feet at about four hundred miles per hour. It's just a guess." He rubbed his face vigorously. "I've been studying this film too hard. Tell me, why California?"

"David didn't say. He just gave me an address in a

place called Weed. He said the answer's there." She massaged his shoulders. "I think you need a break. And I have the perfect suggestion of what we can do about it."

"What do you have in mind?"

She took him by the hand and brought him over to the bed. "I think you have a pretty good idea."

She removed his shirt, unbuttoned his pants and they eased on the bed and entwined their arms and legs together. They kissed passionately and undressed each other fully; making love for the next few hours into the early morning. Les eventually turned off his computer and they drifted off to sleep. He kissed her ear. "I may not know where I'm going, but I sure like getting there."

"Good night, baby."

The next morning they had breakfast and resumed their journey west. They entered the southern border of Wyoming where the sky was a cloudless blue and the weather was much cooler. They passed through Laramie and then Rock Springs, leaving the state without even stopping for gas. They watched the sides of the road for farm houses, but nothing resembled the one in the film. From there they entered Utah and saw the upcoming city of Salt Lake in the distance. It was all dessert from there to Nevada where Les had noticeably become more agitated.

"What's the matter?"

He pointed to the open miles of cactus. "This is Harry's state."

"So that's what's on your mind. You don't have to

worry about that. We're two agricultural agents on our way to California."

"I guess Harry's pretty far south."

"You got to remember, Harry's just one player in Nevada."

They stopped in Winnemucca, devoured a hamburger at a small fast food stand and continued on the road to Reno when Les noticed a police car in the rear view mirror catching up fast. He traveled the speed limit, hoping the trooper would just pass them by. When the police car caught up to them, it matched their speed and followed close behind. Les became extremely nervous and kept slowing down and speeding up.

"Relax. We haven't done anything wrong."

"He's right behind me."

Suddenly the red and blue lights flashed and Les almost urinated in his pants. "Les, we're FDA agents, remember?" She removed a gun from her purse.

"Do we really need that thing?"

"You never know."

Les stepped on the breaks and pulled off to the side of the road. The police car stopped behind him and the trooper remained in his vehicle for what seemed like an eternity. The trooper emerged and walked over to the driver's window and bent down. "Is there a problem, officer?"

"Can I see some ID?"

"Sure." Les handed him his identification.

"FDA, huh?"

"Yeah. On our way to California."

He peered over at Melanie, whose hand tightly

gripped her gun. "You're right brake light is out. Saw it when you left town. Better get it fixed when you get to Reno."

"Sure. Thanks, officer. We'll do that."

"Professional courtesy. No ticket."

"Thanks." He eyed the trooper in the side view mirror as he walked back to the police car. Les started up the car and proceeded down the highway.

"See, Harry doesn't own the cops. And you can bet that Nevada's the last place Harry thinks we're in."

"Damn tail light."

"We'll get the bulb replaced."

"We should spend the night in Reno. I need the rest."

They checked into a wood planked motel just east of Reno's main drag. They ate a simple meal of meat and potatoes at a local café and retired to the room to investigate more footage. Les set up the lap top on a desk below a cheap print of an old west gun fight. He entered the file name. "Let's get a good look at that farmer. Maybe there's something with him."

"He sure is a strange looking fellow."

Les chuckled. "Got to be an alien."

"What are we looking for?"

"Heritage. Maybe a label on his clothes. My initial scans didn't find anything. But I didn't look that close before."

He focused in on the farmer, whose facial features included a lengthy half mooned curvature, pocked bulbous nose and a stretched out pointy chin. "What nationality is this guy, Les?"

"Beats me. He could be from anywhere."

"Perhaps European descent   Could be Italian, French, maybe Spanish."

"I don't know. His face is not going to tell us anything. Let's scan his overalls for a label. Maybe we'll get lucky." Les carefully manipulated the mouse around the still shots of the farmer's clothes. "Nothing. No labels, no rings on his fingers. Nothing that indicates where he's from or where he buys his rags."

"Damn, it's frustrating. Other than the three letters on the barn, there's no other clue. We're running out of options."

"I'm not giving up that easy, Mel. There's got to be something."

"What's left? We've studied this film over and over."

"The only thing left is a small hill in the distance between the barn and the farmer. I've zoomed in on that several times. Nothing there but a few horses and a blank sky."

"Can you zoom in closer to the hill? Maybe we can identify what breed of horse. Or maybe there's a sign out there on the hill."

"Any closer and it gets too blurry. This is about the best I can do without losing the frame's integrity. We don't really have a clear picture of the horses."

"This film is as much a mystery as when we first got it."

He closed his eyes. "I've been staring at the screen for so long my eyes are falling out. Maybe we'll get some answers in Weed."

"It's been a tough day. Let's get some rest. Come to bed and I'll give you a message."

"That sounds really good right about now."

They awoke next morning, glommed down an early breakfast and drove out of Reno towards the California town of Doyle along highway 395. They passed a few highway patrol vehicles and stopped for gas in the town of Susanville. From there they turned on highway 44 that crossed interstate 5, a major California highway. Their route along the interstate took them through patches of sparse vegetation, pine trees and sloping green valleys; eventually moving into the Shasta National Forest.

When they entered the town of Shasta, a highway sign indicated the mileage to Weed. They stopped at a gas station and Les walked into to the little market and purchased a couple of grape drinks. "Excuse me; I'm looking for an Everclear Road?"

"Sure. Go up a few streets, turn right at Anderson and that will take you right there. You can only turn left."

"Thanks." Les returned to the car. "What was that address?"

"2735 Everclear."

"I know the way. We're close." Les stepped on the gas and drove up to Anderson and made a right turn.

"I'm getting jumpy."

"You, Melanie?" Les noticed the Everclear street sign and turned left onto a single lane paved road. They proceeded up and down several hills and didn't see any houses. When they finally saw the first house, Les stopped the car. "2482. Must be up a ways." They began to see other homes that were spread well apart from each other. Les slowed the car when the numbers neared their target. "There it is. 2735." He turned off onto the shoulder of the road.

They stared guardedly at a wooden house with an overgrown grassy front yard, dirt driveway and shabby porch. "Looks like nobody's home, Les."

"What do we do?"

"Looks like we got an old fashion stake out."

"We're going to wait. How long?"

She crumpled her mouth. "How the hell should I know? Pull up there and turn around and park. We'll get a more advantageous view."

He drove the car up the road, turned around slowly and parked the car. He shut off the motor and it was so quiet, a fly battering the back window seemed louder than usual. An hour passed by before the first vehicle appeared on the road. It passed right by them and then there was silence again. A pick up truck motored by, followed by a small sedan as another hour passed uneventfully. Les was getting anxious and Melanie tried to relieve the boredom with small talk. Three hours had passed when a station wagon approached, slowed down and turned into the driveway at 2735.

"Now we're talking.."

They watched intently as a woman and a small boy exited the station wagon and walked towards the front porch. Stupefied, Melanie grabbed Les by the arm and squeezed tight.

His jaw dropped. "Do you know who that is?"

"I sure do. Abel Crawley's widow and son."

"She and the kid would be much older. Like forty to fifty years older. They must be the copies."

"Son of a bitch. David led us right to them."

"Question is; what are they?"

She gazed at him with a purpose. "We'll just have to find out."

He practically jumped out of his seat. "And how do you suggest we do that?"

"We're going to knock on the door."

"Are you nuts? We're going to go right up there and just say, excuse me, what planet are you from?"

She swiveled around and faced him sternly. "Think about it, they're benevolent or malevolent. Either way, we got nothing to lose. We have a film that's not telling us anything. And we have a world that's heading for disaster. I got the mob after me, you the FBI. Maybe they'll give us some answers. We'll either find out the truth or get vaporized. That's better than never knowing."

"No it's not. I'm staying put."

"Fine." She opened the door.

As she passed in front of the windshield, Les pounded the dashboard. "Wait up! I'm going, too." He slammed his door, inhaled the fresh mountain air with eyes closed and followed her up the walkway and onto the porch steps, which creaked as they climbed up to the front door.

Les held his breath as Melanie knocked on the tattered screen door. A woman, obscured by a dusty screen, stood at the threshold. "Can I help you?"

"Are you Mrs. Abel Crawley?"

The woman opened the screen door and peeked out. "Who are you?"

"My name is Melanie Blake and this is Les Palmer.

You and your son bear a striking resemblance to Abel's Crawley's family."

Palmer's tongue stuck dry against his palette. "Please let us in. We've come a long way."

She hesitated, opened the door and stood aside. Melanie walked in first as the boy stood eerily motionless in the middle of the living room. Although young, he spoke with a maturity beyond his age. "You have questions about the farm?"

"Yes", she answered excitedly. "We've been studying the film.

The woman gestured towards an old, frayed couch. "Please sit down."

"Thank you. So are you that woman?"

"Not exactly. At least in your understanding."

"But you did know Abel Crawley?"

She smiled at Melanie. "We are not Mr. Crawley's wife and son. That must be obvious to you. We have not aged."

"So you're copies?"

"No. It is true we share certain genetic traits. But we are not clones. We are not duplicates."

Les scratched his nose. "Yeah, I know. I'm a technician of sorts. I made that determination when studying Crawley's old family films."

Melanie interrupted. "But you are extraterrestrials?"

Les held his breath as the woman smiled warmly. "Our nature is to respect all life forms for their unique individuality. It would be callous of us to simply clone your species. We only required near perfection to assume our roles."

Les blinked nervously. "Are the Crawley's still alive?"

"They are alive and well."

"Where are they?"

The young boy approached them. "That question must be answered in the film we assume you posses."

"We've been studying it."

Melanie almost smiled from the edges of her mouth. "Can you tell us the location of the farm?"

"We can not. You must find that yourselves. But the time is short."

Remaining calm under difficult circumstances, Les folded his hands on his lap. "You'll have to excuse me. It's not everyday I meet visitors from outer space. If you can't tell us why you're here, can you tell us if the earth is in danger?"

"That is another question we are unable to answer to your satisfaction."

"What Les really wants to know is if you're hostile invaders."

The woman hesitated, and then spoke. "We are not able to give you that kind of information. What you're really asking is if we are good or evil; or pose a danger to your planet."

"I don't think we'd be having this conversation if you were hostile. We'd just like a few answers about the destiny of our planet."

"Melanie Blake, this is your world and no one can justify taking it from your species. I can only tell you that we have a purpose and that is why we are here."

She lowered her head sadly. "We got no place to

go. We know we're destroying ourselves. I can't stop that. But maybe you could help us."

The boy reached up and touched her forehead gently. "We apologize. We know you are good people. It is regrettable that so few can harm so many. Your world is not unique in that way. Your species must determine its own survival." He faced away from them. "You must leave now."

Les stood up. "How do you know we won't go to the authorities?"

The woman held out her hands. "Young man, your species is no threat to us."

Melanie grabbed his shoulder. "Come on. We got to go."

Les walked out onto the porch with Melanie in tow. As she stepped onto the deck, the woman called out. "Stop." The woman stared at the boy, who nodded in return. She smiled at Melanie. "Cabler."

"What?"

"Cabler."

Excitement rushed through her body. "Thank you. Thank you."

Melanie strutted joyfully towards the car. Les could not understand her elation. "What the hell's with you?"

"Get in the car. I'm driving."

"What's going on?"

"I got the name of the farm." They slammed the car doors shut. "Cabler."

"Are you kidding? That's great." She started the motor. "Why did she tell you that?"

"Must of felt sorry for us. Now it's time to log onto the internet."

"I'll sniff out a wireless."

Once outside of Weed near a town called McCloud, Les received his first internet connection. He typed in Cabler farms and immediately received a hit. "Bingo. Cabler is a big industrial farming operation in Ogallala, Nebraska."

"I think we passed that town on the way."

"They have a fancy home page. Corn. Wheat. You name it, they grow it."

"Setting course for Nebraska."

"Do me one favor, Melanie. Ease off on the pedal. Don't get pulled over. Let's make it to Nebraska in one piece."

"What a lucky break. This is fantastic."

"Fantastic? We just met people from outer space. That's fantastic."

"Now maybe we can get some answers."

"Just how are we going to do that?"

She slapped his arm. "We're agricultural inspectors, remember?"

Exhausted by the time they reached the town of Kimball Nebraska; they rented another motel and immediately went to sleep. Morning came and they showered, dressed in their best clothes and drove towards Ogallala. It was the first day of September and it must have been one hundred degrees with hellish humidity. All along the highway there were farms, but the Cabler farm had yet to show. They perked up when they spotted a sign on the highway that indicated their objective was two miles north.

September 2020

LES STOPPED THE CAR BELOW an expansive overhead banner with the name, 'Cabler Farms Incorporated'. There was a metal security gate and a guard kiosk in the center median dividing two roads. Les inched the car up to the guard and handed him his credentials.

"FDA? Don't see you on the list."

"It's an unannounced visit. A courtesy call. Can you notify somebody we're here?"

He ducked back into the kiosk and made a phone call. "All right." He then pointed at the main building down the road. "Stay to your right and go into the lobby. Check in at the front desk and say you're here to see Mr. Bathwaite."

"Thanks."

Les drove past a few smaller structures and they could see a range of buildings and tall silos beyond that. Melanie gazed around. "This place is a modern operation. Nothing like in the film."

"I know what you mean. But that was a long time ago. Things change." He parked the car in one of the spaces near the main building. "Let's do it."

"Now what ever happens, don't panic."

"Don't worry about me."

"Let me do all the talking."

The receptionist in the lobby smiled at them. "Can I help you?"

Melanie flashed her badge. "FDA to see Mr. Bathwaite."

"Oh yes. Mr. Bathwaite is our vice president. He's

expecting you. His office is just down at the end of this hallway."

Bathwaite's office had a waiting room with a secretary that gestured for them to pass through to his private office door. Bathwaite, a portly bald headed man, stood up to greet them. "Come in, sit down. We didn't expect you until next month."

They stared at each other, and then Melanie spoke up. "Oh, this isn't about that. We're here for a different reason. Our department is doing a survey on the history of agribusinesses such as yours. It's a new pilot program. This is not mandatory, you understand. We'd just like to ask you a few questions."

He seemed confused, but smiled pleasantly. "What would you like to know?"

Les pulled out a hand computer as Melanie prepared to ask the questions. "How did your business get started?"

His shoulders rose up with pride. "We have a fascinating history. The farm was originally homesteaded by Wilson Cabler in 1890. He was a simple farmer who had two sons. It remained a small family farm until Wilson's death in 1922. He left it to his oldest son, Frederick. But Frederick Cabler wasn't really interested in conventional farming like his father, so his younger brother Trenton took over the business. But it was Trenton's son Charley Cabler that first turned it into a first class farming business. Charley was the true genius of the family and is credited with making it the industrial farm that it is today. It was a bad time for farms in 1937, but Charley's sheer grit and determination kept it going. He died in 1972 and his son James Cabler has been the company's CEO ever since."

"Very informative."

"The Cabler farming operation has been feeding the world for decades."

Les thought for a moment. "Tell me, Mr. Bathwaite. You have quite a modern operation here, a lot of state of the art equipment." He pulled out a print he made of the Crawley barn and foreground. "Did a structure like this ever exist here?"

Bathwaite stared at it. "Maybe a hundred years ago."

"But not in 1968?"

"Heavens no. There's nothing left of the old days."

"Are there any other Cabler properties that may have a structure like this?"

"I'm not aware of any."

"You mentioned this Frederick Cabler. Something about him not liking conventional farming?"

Bathwaite inhaled and then pursed his lips. "You might call him the black sheep of the family. Although there never seemed to be any animosity between him and his family. He was a loner. A believer in hydroponics. Mind you, there's nothing wrong with hydroponics. The Egyptians and Babylonians used those techniques. But to a Nebraska farmer like Wilson Cabler, they were kooky ideas."

"I can understand that."

"He never married. Lived the life of a Bohemian, I'd say. Traveled all over Europe and South America. He died in 1950 in Columbia."

"Was he ever successful?"

"Not to my knowledge. There really isn't much we know about him."

Melanie stood up. "Thank you, Mr. Bathwaite. We appreciate your time."

"It was pleasure meeting you both."

They emerged from the lobby and into the heat of the day. "Les, we got to investigate the history of Frederick Cabler."

"You really think it was his farm?"

"Give me the keys. I'm driving. I'm betting there are no other Cabler farms in the United States. And that just leaves us with Frederick."

"That's pretty flimsy."

"I just have a feeling it has everything to do with him."

"Feeling? More like a wild goose chase." He slumped over in his seat. "So where are we off to; Europe? South America?"

She grinned. "Canada."

"Canada?"

"We have a week left on this rental. We need a place to chill for a while. When I left the Bureau I bought a piece of land in British Columbia. When one goes to work for Harry Philer, one better have a safe house. It's a cabin with water, electricity; all the modern conveniences."

"And how do you plan to get there? The borders can be very dangerous places."

"Fly."

"Now I know you're crazy."

"I'm a pilot. We're going by helicopter."

"Wait a minute, wait a minute. I seem to recall you

weren't that good a pilot. And I don't remember you flying helicopters."

"I did for a while. I know what I'm doing."

Les dropped his head forward. "Okay, so you can fly helicopters. Just how are we going to get a helicopter?"

"Steal it."

"Then everybody will be after us."

"I don't think so. We're going to take our helicopter from Harry Philer."

"Forget it."

"When I first went to work for Harry, I knew what kind of person he was. I always had in mind that one day I may need to get some quick transportation."

"So we're just going to go to the Extravaganza, steal a chopper and fly out?"

"Essentially…yes."

"There's got to be an easier way."

"Occasionally Harry has important guests that he personally flies from McCarran to the hotel. He uses his finest bird; a real fancy rig. It's got a range of 425 miles, seats six passengers and has a fully stocked bar."

"We're going to hijack it right under his nose?"

"I installed an access port at the site they generate the holographic UFOs. As chief of security it was easy. Only my codes work."

"They'll detect it like your phony power failure."

"Not this time. These entry ports are for low priority systems. I scrambled all the inquiries, so my codes will be hidden. Les, I know what I'm doing."

Exasperated, Les opened up his lap top and waited for the next wireless connection. "In for a penny, in for a pound. Let's see what we can find on this Frederick Cabler. Here it is. Not much. It refers to him as a member of the Cabler farming family. Directs me to the Cabler site. And we already know that stuff."

"Are there any other significant Cabler farming families?"

"Nothing. I guess there could be a lone farmer named Cabler somewhere. But not listed on the search engine."

"None the less, the alien woman told us the name was Cabler. And that jives with the last three letters on the barn."

He raised his eyebrows. "There's one other thing. I'm pretty sure the big tree in the footage is an oak. It looks like an oak, and I remember something about oak trees growing in the northern regions of South America."

"Frederick Cabler died in Columbia."

"I'm not ready to take that leap of faith."

Harry Philer puffed on a cigar in his office while chatting on the phone to his mobster friend, Karl. "What do you mean you can't find her?"

"I got feelers everywhere. Even contacted my Mexican friends."

"She and Palmer can't just disappear."

"I'm not saying we won't find them. But it's a big country."

He choked on a cloud of smoke. "That bitch has my film."

"Harry, she's got to contact you for ransom."

"I'm not so sure, my friend. I make a lot of money on that film. But if it ever got out, it would be useless.

She knows that and has probably made copies anyway. I don't think her intentions are for ransom."

"She'll make a mistake. We'll get her."

The night time Nevada sky contained as many stars and streaking meteors as dark spaces. Les steered the car tiredly through the desert at various speeds, yawning and trying to stay awake. Melanie warned him that the side road they needed to take was only a few miles up the highway. When they came upon it, he turned on the narrow, badly paved surface. The car bounced and pitched for about ten miles until the road turned into a dirt surface, which really knocked them around. She told him to stop next to a thicket of spindly trees and shut off the motor. With the exception of boisterous crickets, the place was as remote as one could imagine.

"Where the heck are we?"

"Sniff that desert sage. God, I love it."

"What are we doing here?"

"This road's near the hotel. It's not access road. Nobody ever goes on it, especially at night. But it's close enough to the holographic site for me to hike to it in the morning."

"So what do we do for now?"

"Sleep. The employees stay up until about four in the morning and then rest most of the day in the air conditioning. I'm going it alone. I know the way in and I know where the ground sensors are. This place has better security than some of the areas on the hotel grounds."

"Philer doesn't want any hikers stumbling on his fake bullshit."

"No doubt." She leaned over and laid her head on

his shoulder. "Let's just enjoy the night along with the crickets and coyotes."

He stroked her hair. "You think these aliens are everywhere."

"Who knows? We don't even know what they want."

"Just think, a few weeks ago all I had to worry about was the end of the world. And now I'm preoccupied with the whole universe."

"Isn't that what you always wanted from life?"

He yawned broadly. "Yeah, it's loads of fun."

The morning came with gnats buzzing around Palmer's nose. He woke up rubbing his nostrils and waving them off. "Good morning."

"Oh, my breath. I wish I had some mints."

"How about some water?"

"She stretched out her arms. I'd better get going. It's going to take me an hour to get there. Hand me the lap top."

Melanie trotted down the dirt road until the car vanished from her sight. She hiked haphazardly down a hillside, using the brush as cover. She avoided the sharper cactus, all the while wiping the perspiration accumulated from the blazing morning sun. She climbed over a ridge, surveyed the unfolding landscape and plunged downward with side slipping precision. She almost lost her balance a few times, but regained control, holding the computer tight against her stomach. At the bottom was a dry river bed that she followed for a quarter mile until reaching the hill that separated her from the holographic saucer site.

She climbed up the steep cliff, grabbing onto

anchored rocks with one arm while holding the computer with the other. At the summit she squinted from the reflection off the metal and concrete buildings below. She crisscrossed down the hill to avoid the ground sensors and took agonizingly slow steps towards the side of one of the buildings that had an attached electrical panel.

Melanie was three feet away from the panel when she heard the front door of the building crack open. She stood transfixed, unable to determine which way the employee would turn. She held her breath as the man walked straight out the door, unzipped his pants and urinated on the dirt. She had no idea why he would not just use the interior restroom; and if he were to turn to the left and walk to the side, she would certainly be discovered. Melanie silently pressed against the side of the building and held her breath as the man went back inside and shut the door.

She removed the power panel, plugged in the computer terminal and entered her secret code. Within seconds, the downloading process began and two minutes later she was finished. She returned the panel into its place, tucked the computer under her arm and climbed back up the hillside. She hastened her steps, confident that she had the necessary information.

Les watched the rear view mirror and was relieved when he saw her coming up the road. He started the motor and she got inside. "How did it go?"

"Perfect. I got everything."

"Where to?"

"A little town called Ely. We'll check into a motel

and see what we got. With any luck, we should be able to move within a week."

"Luck is all we got these days."

"Turn right on the highway and head north."

Ely was a solitary, dusty town with a clean cinderblock motel that suited them well. After checking in, Melanie showered first, eager to wash off the dirt that darkened the floor of the tub. As Les showered, Melanie turned on the computer and scanned the information. Les came out with a towel draped around his waist. "Find anything?"

"We're in luck."

"What do you have?"

"Three days from now Harry is expecting Mr. and Mrs. Stoddard of Boston fame. They are prominent and Harry will be meeting them personally in Vegas. They have a private jet."

"I still don't like this. We should just hoof it over to Canada?"

"We don't have that much time. Trust me, this is the best way. Harry's not going to rest until he kills us. This is the only way. We're pushing against time and we may not have enough left."

"I still get this nagging feeling you're playing me."

"I did lie to you about some things. David visited me one year before I first told you he did. I even knew that Harry would find out about the electronic intrusion sooner than I said he would. And without you, hijacking Harry's chopper along with Harry himself would have been unnecessary because I wouldn't have had the film. But I am telling you the truth that having you back in my personal life is the best thing that every happened.

I should have come clean from the beginning. I'm sorry for that."

He gazed at her with a blank expression, and then he began to smile. "Typical Melanie Blake. But what we've been through trumps any other considerations now. I met aliens and we have real UFO documentation. I'm in all the way. But if there are any other surprises, please tell me now?"

"No, that's it. But now comes the hardest part. Getting to our safe house. If you ever wanted to be a secret agent, here's your chance. The last thing Harry's ever going to expect is us coming to him."

"Life's never dull with you."

"Tomorrow you'll go to the local hardware store and buy some rope, a screwdriver and twenty planks of wood one inch thick, twelve inches long and four inches wide. And a battery charged drill kit. I'll find some flattened steel hooks."

The following morning after donuts and coffee, Les purchased the necessary items Melanie had ordered. She found a little two man machine shop and was able to have custom steel hooks fabricated to her specific measurements. They met back at the motel and Les spilled out all the items on the bed. "Good job. So I guess it's time to let you in on all the details."

"That would be nice."

"The wood planks serve as a makeshift ladder. The rope obviously binds the planks. The hooks are to grab the edges of an exhaust vent. I wrote the book on the security at the Extravaganza. Now they've changed all the codes and protocols by now. But I basically know the weaknesses. One of them is the grounds. The hotel security is excellent, but Extravaganza is still a business. Guests can walk freely in and out the front doors. And while there's an eight foot perimeter wall and cameras; there are a few blind spots. There are only two structures not connected to the main hotel; the vehicle pool and the aircraft hangar. Of course they have armed guards in each department, but that won't matter to us. When they built the structures, they ran the exhaust vents under the grounds and up to the area near the perimeter wall. They didn't want roof exhaust to drift over to the hotel."

"So we're going to crawl through the vents?"

"Exactly. There are three vents that extend underground out to the grass. They protrude about five feet above the ground. The grills face the wall and I loosened the screws on one of them. So the vent grill is only wedged up against the vent surface. No one questions the head of security wherever they go."

"What if they found it and fixed it?"

"Then we do it your way. We walk across the Canadian border."

"And the cordless drill?"

"That will come in handy once we're in. Now there's two ways I could have stolen the helicopter. The riskier would be to somehow hide out in the chopper and surprise the pilots the next morning. But so many things could go wrong. Fortunately for us, Harry is an egotistical bastard with delusions of being a five star general. His pilots don't dress like commercial pilots would. No, they have custom orange jump suits with high tech helmets. Harry loves to show off." She tossed two vinyl duffle bags onto the bed; one larger than the other. She opened her suitcase and brought out two pistol sized dart guns, each containing a liquid substance. "A nasty little surprise I got from one of my former friends. One shot of this and you're out in seconds."

"Is it lethal?"

"No. Just puts you out a few hours."

"So you're now James Bond."

"We stuff the ladder in the big bag and the rest in the smaller. It's time to make the ladder. You ready for arts and crafts?"

"When it comes to you, I'm ready for anything."

"Tomorrow we'll shop for some dark clothes and rubber soled shoes. And then as the saying goes, we'll rock and roll it."

Two days later and the evening before they would infiltrate the Extravaganza, Melanie rolled up the ladder into the large bag. She carefully placed all their money and gold coins in the smaller bag, along with the dart guns, her semi-automatic pistol and his small revolver. "Shouldn't one of us carry a gun?" he asked.

"If we're forced to use our weapons at the Extravaganza, security will probably cut us down pretty quick."

"That's comforting."

"Besides, I remember you shoot about as well as I fly a helicopter."

"We're about to die, and you're making jokes."

"Les, this is no joke. You got to psyche yourself. I need you to concentrate the whole time. I know you can do it."

"You can count on me. I'm in all the way."

They tossed the two duffle bags in the car and dumped all the rest of their clothes into the trash can behind the motel. They traveled south towards the Extravaganza and turned onto a side road near the hotel where they ditched the car behind a clump of creosote bushes. It was almost a moonless night and it was very dark when the headlamps went off. They gathered the bags and Les slapped the hood of the car. "It's like leaving an old friend."

"Let's hope it's the last time we see it."

Les shook his head. "In a couple of days it will be a stolen vehicle."

"The hotel's two miles in that direction."

They hiked over a relatively flat stretch of land until reaching the perimeter wall. They set the bags down. "What, no barbed wire? No electrified fence?"

"I told you it's not a prison. But this specific location has about a three foot blind spot between two cameras. This is where we go over." She removed the rope ladder, tossed the hooks up to the top and yanked them tight. "I'll go first. Hand me the other bag." She climbed to the top, glanced around and then signaled for Les to come up. She sat next to him. "You'll have to jump."

"Down there?"

"You can hang off the side."

"Yeah, that's better."

Once he was on the ground, she loosened the hook and tossed the ladder over the side. She jumped down next to him and they stood in a grassy area amidst several trees and vegetation. "Okay, the vent's over there."

"No sensors?"

"Nope. Let's go." They ran up to the metallic vent grill. "Give me the twine." She tied a knot on each side of the edge of the grill and then she jimmied the grill off with the screwdriver. "Nothing to it."

They carefully set the grill on the ground against the vent shaft and placed the ladder hooks over the side. Once the ladder rungs dropped through the interior of the vent, she gestured for him to climb down twenty feet to the bottom. After climbing down two rungs, she pulled the grill up by the tweed and wedged it back into position. Although the hooks impeded the grill from fitting perfectly flat, they were thin enough to fool anyone passing by. She then climbed down the ladder and joined him at the bottom of the duct. She tied the smaller bag to her ankle. "Feel all that warm rushing air and mechanical noises down there? They won't hear us in the vehicle pool or the hangar." They're always working twenty four hours a day. They won't notice us making any noise."

"What about the ladder?"

"Leave it. We might have to use it if the plan fails. Leave the big bag, too."

"It's roomier than I thought in here."

"I'm glad you don't have claustrophobia."

She aimed her flashlight down the horizontal section of the duct and began crawling with the bag in tow. Les followed her about one hundred and fifty feet until they reached the first right corner which led to a long straight passage. As they traversed the duct they heard banging hammers, electric motors and talkative mechanics. Up ahead was the first sign of light filtering through a vent grill. She turned around to him. "Remember to stay as quiet as possible."

Les peeked through each vent hole at the busy mechanics in the brightly lit room. After crawling the entire distance of the vehicle pool they entered the adjacent aircraft hangar. Each time they passed by a vent grill, Les could see the helicopters lined up and being attended by the mechanics. They rounded another corner at the end of the hangar and stopped at a narrower intersecting duct. Melanie crawled to the edge of the grill, opened up the bag, removed the drill and twisted a screwdriver bit inside.

"I came here a while back, removed these screws and put a slit in the ends of them for this very moment."

"Naturally. You think of everything."

"It's going to get a little noisy. But nobody's in this room. It's the pilot's locker."

"I can still hear the machinery."

"It should cover us." She stuck the screwdriver into the first screw and it pushed it through onto the floor of the locker room. She repeated the process three more times and pushed the vent onto the floor below. They both leaped out and Melanie picked up the vent and tightened back the screws. "Linen closet's over there. Let's get inside."

"Now what?"

"We got about six hours before the pilots arrive. I suggest we pile a few of those towels and make ourselves comfortable. It's going to be pitch black in here."

While Les stacked the towels, Melanie removed the two dart pistols, inspected them thoroughly and shut off the closet light. She shined her flashlight on the bag and removed black duct tape and twine and set it on the ground.

"I'm only going to get one shot at these guys."

"You'll get them. You're James Bond."

Hours passed and they heard voices entering the locker room. Every nerve in Les' body tingled as Melanie stood up with a pistol in each hand. She carefully turned the closet door knob and opened it a crack as both pilots stood in front of the sinks, removed their shirts and stared into the mirrors. She knew they might see her for a split second, but was confident their proximity to each other made for an easy shot. She held her breath, kicked open the door and startled both men. She fired the left gun first, and then the right; sending both men crashing to the floor unconscious.

"Come on, Les. We don't have much time."

They dragged the pilots over to the closet; duct taped them, gagged them, opened the lockers and removed two orange flight suits and helmets.

"Now what do we do?"

"Put on the helmets on and walk outside. I know pilots, and normally they would carry their helmets; but we can't afford to do that. We need to wear the damn things. So I'm relying on the fact that most people don't notice things when they're doing routine tasks. When you do the same job day after day, you become complacent."

"That may be true. But what if we're stopped?"

"I doubt we'll get stopped. But if it does happen, just wave them off. You got your gun, right? Worse comes to worry, we just leave without Harry."

"I got my gun. I just hope I don't have to use it."

They dropped the helmets snugly over their heads and pulled the tinted visors down over their eyes. Frightened and uncertain, Les followed Melanie out into the hangar where they passed several mechanics that didn't even look up to notice them. The helicopter was already prepared on the tarmac for lift off and a ground crewman waved at them as they passed each other on the way out.

Melanie opened the side door of the helicopter and Les jumped up inside. She walked around the nosecone, opened the pilot's door and hoped into the seat. She initiated the start up sequence and turned off the transponder. The jet engines began to whine, the blades started to rotate and she gazed back at Les. "When Harry steps in, aim that gun at him and threaten his life. Don't let anybody else in."

"Will do."

On cue, Harry and his guards meandered out to the helicopter. Les waited for them, holding his gun down against the side of his leg. When Harry lifted his foot up to the first step, Les pointed the gun at his head. "Get in!"

"Whoa…what is this?"

"Get in or I'll blow your head off."

"The guard pulled out his weapon and Harry stifled him. "Don't shoot!"

"Tell him to back off or you're dead."

Harry complied, the guard backed away, Les yanked him inside and the helicopter wildly lurched off the tarmac and flew away from the hotel erratically. Les closed the sliding door as Melanie aimed her menacing pistol at him. "Don't anything stupid, Harry."

"Melanie Blake. I can't believe it."

"I heard you were looking for me."

Les looked at Melanie while aiming his gun at Philer. "Won't they follow?"

"It will take about fifteen to twenty minutes before they get to another chopper. But we'll be long gone and they don't know what direction we're going in because I'm heading north in a few minutes. I'm going to fly low and stay clear of military space. Harry's other helicopters couldn't keep up with us if they tried."

Philer straightened out his tie. "You got the film, why do you need me?"

"Not for ransom, that's for damn sure."

"So this is Les Palmer, boy genius."

"At your service."

"You know kid, she's using you. She uses everybody."

"Shut up, Philer."

"She's going to kill me, and when that's done, she'll get rid of you, too."

Melanie looked back. "Save it, Harry. We're in love."

"Yeah, love. That lasts a long time with you."

"Don't do anything stupid. Les will shoot if he has to."

"I'll be on my best behavior."

With both hands tightly on the control sticks, she steered the helicopter at high speeds over barren hills and rock piled gullies. Well on a northern route, she throttled down to fifty miles per hour and aimed the nosecone towards a narrow plateau overhanging a steep cliff on one side and a gradual slope on the other. She pulled back on the vertical controls and landed roughly on the flattened dirt surface. She shut off the engine, kicked open her door, went around to the side door, waved her gun and pulled Harry out. "Let's go." She jabbed the gun into his side and pushed him to the edge of the cliff.

Les shouted. "What are you doing?"

Harry peered over her shoulder. "She's going to kill me, kid. And you're next."

"Melanie, don't!"

She smiled at Harry. "You son of bitch. You sent Karl after me."

"What did you expect? You stole my film."

"You don't know anything, and you never will."

"Just shoot me and get it over with."

She aimed the gun at his head. "Wait right here, Harry." She walked back to Les. "There's a water jug in under that sink back there. Get it."

Les was relieved she wasn't going to murder him. He gave her the jug and she returned to Philer.

"Don't want you to go thirsty, Harry. It's a big desert. If you head back that way about twenty miles, you should reach a town or two."

"You're going to leave me out here? It's a hundred degrees."

"Good luck, Harry. You're going to need it."

She returned to the helicopter, started up the engines and lifted off the plateau, stranding Harry. Les sat up in the co-pilot's chair. "What's going to happen to him?"

"I pointed him in the right direction. If he follows

that, he'll be okay. But he'll probably think I'm lying and go the other way."

"Damn it, Melanie. This was always your plan, wasn't it?"

"Les, he sent a butcher after me. We would have never been truly safe, wherever we went."

"I can't help but thinking that I might next."

"You know that's not true. I would never harm you."

He slowly smiled. "I guess you could have got rid of me at any time during the last few weeks. So, where to now?"

"We have enough gas to get us to Burley, Idaho. We'll only need one more refueling at a little place called Sandpoint near the Canadian border."

"They won't be looking for Harry's chopper?"

"Everybody hates the man. And as far as his people at the Extravaganza are concerned, they're not going to make that much of an effort. The consortium has a hierarchy and the hotel business will go on."

"Your flying skills are better than I remember."

"This thing practically flies itself.'

Les gazed downward as they swiftly moved over the terrain of sand and sage. "You are amazing, Melanie. I can't believe we actually stole a helicopter."

Cursing Melanie at the top of his lungs, Harry picked up the jug of water, glanced around and headed in the opposite direction she had advised. He stumbled awkwardly down the gradually sloping side of the plateau, swigged from the water jug at the base of a dry river bed and immediately backed into a chollo cactus. He grabbed at the sharp needles in his leg and cursed Melanie even louder. He limped along in pain, constantly brushing away pesky flies that landed on his face and forehead.

Harry kept swigging gulps of water, disregarding any kind of rationing for such a long trek. His stomach ached violently and diarrhea dripped down each leg of his pants. He kept cursing Melanie until his throat swelled and eyes throbbed. The flies kept buzzing about him and the afternoon sun blurred his vision. He often stopped to rest and scratch at the dried excrement inside his pants. Walking soon became unbearable with his infected cactus wound and swollen feet.

Reaching a dead end of boulders blocking his path, he knew he'd have to climb up and around them. He mustered every bit of strength, clung onto the protruding hillside rocks and hoisted himself upward. He fell down several times, all the while fending off multitudes of flies and what appeared to be a chain of ticks gathering around his ankles. Soaked with perspiration, he reached the summit of the hill, grabbed for a loose rock, squished a stink beetle under his hand and dropped the water jug that emptied onto the ground.

"NO!" He sobbed uncontrollably.

A wasp landed on his hand and he clenched his fist over it, screaming as it stung him. Still holding the dead wasp, he stared at the empty dessert, unwilling to go on any further. Deliriously indecisive, he plodded along in an arbitrary direction, each step as if a knife was stabbing his foot. He was so thirsty he picked off a piece of rotting prickly pear cactus, only to spit out the sour juice. As the hot sun pounded his face, he failed to heed the warning of a nearby rattlesnake. It struck his leg, injected venom and he fell to the ground.

Almost incoherent, he knew the snake was the end of the line for him. But Harry Philer would not die alone. The first buzzard landed on a nearby rock. Another one flapped its wings above his head and landed right next to him. He shouted at them and tried to throw tiny rocks, but they patiently landed three, four and three more. With any luck, Harry would die before they started to feast. Unfortunately for Harry, luck was not on his side that day.

Melanie and Les were twenty minutes away from reaching the Burley airport. Their fuel was low, but they had enough to reach their destination. With the airport in sight,

Melanie contacted a small control tower and was given clearance to land. She set the helicopter down on the tarmac and steered over to the fuel depot. "Les, pull out some cash and give him an extra five hundred dollar tip and a few gold coins. We'll get excellent service."

Les ambled towards the pay booth and stood at the counter. An older man greeted him. "That your bird out there?"

"Yes." Les glanced up at the suspended television set.

"It's a real beauty."

"What's happening in the news?"

"You haven't heard. Some kind of flu hitting Washington and New York."

"Really, what kind of flu?"

"They don't know. Only some people have died."

Les paid the man and gave him the extra funds. "For your kids."

"That's mighty nice of you, but I don't have kids. I do have a golden retriever."

"Then...for your dog."

"We'd be most honored to accept this gift."

Les walked back towards the helicopter as the ground crew finished up. Fully fueled, Melanie started up the engines, maneuvered back out on the tarmac and lifted off. "Some kind of flu hitting the east coast."

"Early for flu season."

"Are you thinking biological attack?"

She flew in a northern direction. "Anything's possible."

The helicopter dipped in and out of green covered hills and valleys on the way to Sandpoint, a small Idaho community fifty miles from the Canadian border. Melanie followed highway 95 below as the terrain turned greener and more mountainous. They sky was cloudier, soon becoming a vast gray tapestry with even darker gray clouds overlapping in front. What would normally be a blue lake was blackened by the ominous skies.

Melanie throttled back power as she made visual contact with the one strip airport ahead. She landed near the refueling station and shut off the engines. She grabbed the bag. "I'm going this time. I took a few helicopter lessons a while back."

"That explains it. Your flying has been too good."

Melanie embraced a woman in white overalls at the doorway of a tiny wooden shack. "How are you, Bridget?"

"Good to see you, Melanie. Been a while. Is that your chopper?"

"A friend's. I need a half a tank."

"My pleasure."

"Bridget, I hear there's some kind of flu going on."

"It's terrorism, if you ask me."

"I'm not surprised."

"Where you heading?"

"Montana. I'd like to stay a while, but I don't have much time." She opened her bag and pulled out a bundle of cash. "This is for you."

"Oh, this is too much."

"Don't worry about it. My boyfriend over there is loaded."

"Well, thank you. And good luck."

After refueling, they lifted off and flew west for a while until Melanie turned them around on a route towards the Canadian border. Skirting the tops of the pine covered mountains; Les gritted his teeth as they almost scraped the upper branches. An hour later and well into Canada, Melanie slowed down to about thirty five miles per hour and flipped a switch to empty the fuel tanks.

"What are you doing?"

"About eight months ago I took a little camping trip and found the perfect spot to ditch. I marked by GPS...and there it is."

"But our fuel?"

"That part's over. We don't need any more fuel."

She eased the nosecone back and hovered over a small open area surrounded by trees on three sides and a cliff on the fourth. She lowered the helicopter slowly as the warning buzzer indicated an empty fuel tank. The landing area was so tight that the spinning blades clipped the sides of the pine branches. She set the helicopter on the ground and kept the engines running and blades twirling.

"Time to get out, Les."

"What are you going to do?"

She pushed a few buttons. "I'm setting the auto pilot." The engine began sputtering due to the low fuel. "Get out, now!" She grabbed the bag, opened the door and jumped out; Les immediately followed. Still sputtering, the helicopter moved forwards and rolled off the side of the cliff, crashing and breaking apart as it disappeared into the thick brush below. A barely visible puff of dust rose from the depths. "That's why I dumped the fuel. They'll never find it."

"Now what do we do?"

"My place is about four days hiking." She looked around and recognized a pile of rocks by a tree trunk. "There it is." She picked up a plastic wrapped shovel from behind the rocks. "Help me dig?"

"You are so prepared. You put the boy scouts to shame."

"Three feet down there's some sleeping bags, pup tents, a stove and freeze dried food. As for water, there's plenty of rivers along the way."

"So we're going camping."

"Hope you're up for it." After digging up the gear, Melanie held a compass in her hand. "That way. It's a lot of stuff to carry, but it's worth it."

At first the terrain was fairly level as they trudged through annoying branches and slippery muddy bogs.

Insects didn't seem to be a problem, but the gravelly sloshing path made for sore ankles. They were stuck by thorns while looking for open areas under the canopy for faster movement. As the sunlight ebbed, Melanie chose a campsite near a fast moving stream. "What more can you ask for? Gather up some firewood and I'll boil some water."

"Are we having steak and caviar tonight?"

"I don't know about steak, but salmon eggs might do. I think we'll settle for goulash. I'll get the propane going."

"Wonderful. I'll gather some wood." He gazed up at the sky. "Do you think it's going to rain?"

"It does rain here during the summer. But I have flint to get the fire going."

Sky dotted stars and far off wolf howls were somehow comforting as their stomachs digested the food. Melanie and Les spread leaves, moss and pine needles over the ground and pitched their single occupant tents. Exhausted with sore legs, they fell asleep and awoke the next morning to a slight chill. Melanie cooked cereal and coffee over the stove and they broke camp to hike for the second day. The ground was steeper and more difficult to navigate than the previous day. Three hours of such demands caused their leg muscles to constrict and their ankles to throb. Soon they discovered another stream and were able to follow an easier path. When the sun began to set on the second day, Melanie selected another campsite where they heard a whisper of rolling thunder.

"Going to rain a little tonight. Always good to carry gortex. We'll stay dry."

"You haven't said anything about bears."

"I didn't want to alarm you, but I did see some scat."

"Are you sure it wasn't mine?"

"I got a rifle; just in case. But I won't have to use it."

"What's for dinner?"

"Chicken and rice."

"My favorite. I can't get enough of freeze dried."

That night it thundered and rained. Les didn't sleep well, worried that a nearby tree would be struck by lightening. It was fortunately a summer downpour and the temperature was mild. The morning arrived with the sun piercing through the cloud covering, giving way to beautiful blue sky. Although the ground was soaked, level ground and a lack of thick brush made it easy to hike.

Les became curious when he spotted a patch of wild raspberries. He went over to pick them but failed to notice a steep decline on the other side. He slipped and tumbled down twenty feet of hillside, scraping his arms until he grabbed onto a fallen tree trunk. Melanie ran over to him. "Are you all right?"

"Yeah. I'm okay."

"You got to be more careful, Les. You could have been injured."

He started up the incline. "I know, I know."

She wiped a trickle of blood off his slightly abraded cheek. "You look all right. That could have easily been a hundred foot cliff." She kissed him quickly. "From now on, stay close to me."

"No problem."

They traveled another full day and found a camp site under a canopy of pines. The collection of dead leaves on the ground made for the most comfortable campsite yet. The sky was still cloudless and Melanie was fairly certain that it wouldn't rain again. They used the flint to ignite a fire, boiled another freeze dried meal and enjoyed a final cup of coffee from the dwindled supply.

"I'm going to miss this."

"To our journey, Les. We've made good time I think we might be home sooner than later."

After hiking for five hours, Melanie began to recognize some of the landmarks near her home. They walked along a well manicured trail and passed several cabins; some puffing out smoke from the chimneys. She could see her house through a clearing and picked up the pace until reaching the driveway. She ran up to the porch, removed a wooden plank near the wall under the front window and held up a hidden key. Once inside, she turned on a flashlight. "No electricity until I start the generator."

"I just want a shower."

"The generator will run for twenty four hours. Tomorrow I'll go into town and get the power reinstated." She opened up an inner door to the garage, flashed the light on her pick up truck and then started the gas generator.

Les waited in the middle of the living room. "Everything okay?"

"Yep. Hot water heater's on. We'll have a shower in about three hours."

"I can't wait."

"Oh, and remember we're Allison and James Dunston."

"So that's who you're known as in these parts."

"One can never be too careful when dealing with Harry Philer." She flicked the light switch in the living room and then went into her bedroom and did the same. She opened a hidden panel that revealed a safe. She spun the combination and pointed to one hundred thousand dollars of Canadian money neatly stored on three shelves."

"You're a good squirrel. Melanie Blake."

"Compliments of Harry. Enough to live on for a long time. That is, if we have a long time."

October 2020

LES ADJUSTED WELL TO HIS new life in Canada. He reclined in a rocker chair in the living room and watched the news on television as Melanie cooked the evening's dinner. The temperatures had fallen dramatically in a short time. A strong crackling fire reflected off the wooden floors as Les closed and opened his fatigued eyes; barely able to follow the news reports. Suddenly he shouted to Melanie, who had just brought the potatoes to boil.

"What's up?"

"Looks like we might be having a Mideast war soon."

"What do you mean?"

"Pakistan, Iran and even Russia's involved."

"Russia is going to join with them?"

"They say they're on the U.S. side."

"Yeah…sure." She went back into the kitchen. "Better turn that stuff off. You'll just get depressed."

The reporter read the teleprompter. "And now on to the mysterious flu strain. It is generally believed this was a biological attack on the citizens of the United States, as well as those in eastern Canada. It appears they have isolated those still infected. The CDC has admitted there may be deadlier mutations of the strain. They claim that all considered, the deaths of 30,000 people are minor compared to what could have if it had mutated. Unfortunately, there continues to be traffic jams and panic along the east coast. We'll keep you informed if anything changes"

"Turn it off, Les. Dinner is served."

He shut off the television and walked into the kitchen where his food steamed off the plate. "You might be right. This may be the end."

"I'm certain of it. Still, I'd like to know why these aliens are here. I guess we've all but given up on finding the farm."

"Defeatist? That doesn't sound like you."

"Don't get me wrong. Even though we've exhausted all the clues from the Crawley film, I might just head off to Columbia to look for it."

He was distressed. "Doesn't sound like a wise decision. You don't even know if it's Frederick Cabler."

"He died in Columbia in 1950. That's as big a clue as anything from the film."

He dropped his fork on the table. "It's a needle in a haystack."

"You said yourself; maybe the world's coming to an end."

"Melanie, is Canada such a bad place to settle down?"

She gazed at him with an expression of consternation. "It's a beautiful place. But what good is it if this is truly the end?"

"We could spend what time we have left with each other."

"That's sweet. But I'm not ready to give up just yet."

"I'll keep scanning the film. But I don't think there's anything there."

"Tomorrow we'll go into town and I'll sign the property deed over to you."

He pushed the plate away. "Sounds like you've already made your decision."

"I'm just being a realist."

The next morning Melanie was true to her word and drove Les to the hall of records and signed over the property deed. They shopped for items in town and bought steaks, a case of beer, two bottles of wine and some weather stripping for the master bedroom windows. Melanie was disturbingly sullen and Les tried to lighten up the mood with jokes. When they arrived home, Les didn't go to the television set as usual, but opened up his lap top on the antique roll top desk.

Melanie put the steaks in the refrigerator and then walked into the living room. "What are you doing?"

"I haven't looked at this for a while."

"Not giving up. I like that."

"I owe it to you. You want this farm so bad."

"But we've been over it so many times."

"There's got to be something we missed."

She patted his shoulder. "My little optimist."

"To be honest, I really didn't want to find that damn farm. I know I'm being selfish. But I'm not up to another long journey." He giggled. "Think about it. Three weeks ago, I was a happy FBI guy. Now I'm living like a happy hermit."

"Okay 'G' man, let's see if you can find something new on the film."

"Anything for James Bond."

"What should we look for?"

"Since we haven't scanned it for a while, let's take a whole new gander. Like it's the first time we've even seen it."

"I'm game."

"I'll run it in slow motion. Here we go. There's the trees. Here comes the saucer into view." He stopped the action. "Zooming in on the saucer. Burnished rough metallic with tree leaves behind it. The shadow is consistent with a real object. No discernable markings on the vessel. Still looking for that sign, 'apples for ten cents'.

"Wouldn't that be nice?"

"Eucalyptus trees. Those trees can grow a lot of places. No carvings on the big tree bark or any other carvings."

She pointed. "Oh look, Melanie loves Les."

"How could I have missed that?"

"Here comes the farmer and the barn."

"The big headed farmer of unknown origin. You'd

think that big face would have some kind of scars or something."

"He's got plenty of wrinkles."

He scanned away from the farmer and focused on the entirety of the farm. "I'm taking another run from the saucer in front of the Eucalyptus trees, the distant hills with the horses, the bloated farmer head, the barn…" He froze.

"What? You look like you've just seen a ghost."

He cocked his head. "That's funny. You look at something a thousand times and don't stop to think about it. The mind works that way. You tend to eliminate little details. Kind of like those mechanics not noticing us in the hangar."

"What did we miss?"

"We keep saying distant hill. All the rest of the footage has perspective to judge size and distance, but that stupid hill doesn't have any references. It only appears for a couple of seconds; and there's nothing to tell us how far it is, or how high it is."

"Why does that matter, Les?"

His head jerked upward. "What if that hill isn't that far away? What if it's a little out of focus because it's nearby background? Cameras work that way."

"Why would that make any difference? There's still no signs or anything. Just a few horses."

He sat amazed with an exaggerated nod. "Horses? All the time it's been staring at us in the face. How do we know they're horses?"

"What else could they be?"

He zoomed in on the hill. "The two animals on the right are too blurry to discern. They could be horses, but without perspective they could be any animal. Now, look at the one on the left. It's still fuzzy, out of focus. But whatever it is, it's facing directly at the camera."

"Yeah, so?"

"Melanie, check out that neck. It's too long to be a horse. Let me try to focus in better. There, that's the best I can do. I don't think that thing's a horse."

"Well it's not an ostrich."

"No, it's too bulky and has too much hair." He grabbed her arm. "That's a llama."

Her eyes were transfixed. "You're right."

"And if those are llamas, then we're probably in South America."

"Frederick Cabler."

"Now wait a minute, Melanie. Columbia's a big country. And we already know there's no information about Frederick Cabler in Columbia."

"It's his place. I know it."

"Cabler died in 1950, right? So the new owners just kept the fading Cabler sign up on the barn for eighteen years until Crawley finds it?"

"Apparently so. The farm's in Columbia. Abel Crawley was a traveler and he went to South America."

Les covered his face and moaned. "You really don't want to go to Columbia?"

"We have to go. That's where the farm is"

"Melanie, we're in Canada for goodness sakes. We're so far from South America. How the hell are we going to get there?"

"You're forgetting, I'm good at this kind of thing. Les, the world's coming to an end. We got nothing here but death. If there is any chance of survival, we got to go to Columbia and find that farm."

"You're not thinking rationally. Harry's got to be dead. The FBI, even when they discover I'm gone, is going to be preoccupied about what's happening all over. They won't even care about me. Both of us are free to live here and enjoy what's left."

She turned away from him. "You're the one being irrational. We have an opportunity to make something of our lives. Maybe out there in the universe. That woman in Weed California gave me that name for a reason."

He stood up and clutched onto her from behind with a bear hug. "Let's sleep on this and talk about it tomorrow."

She swung around. "There's nothing to talk about. We solved the mystery of the film. We know where the farm is."

"This is nuts. It's dangerous enough in the states, let alone South America. Survival's going to be impossible."

"I'll protect you, Les. I always have."

"And who's going to protect you?"

"We've been through so much. We can get through this."

That night Les laid down next to Melanie in bed with open eyes and gritted teeth. He had a big decision to make, one that could alter their relationship forever. In his heart he knew the world was probably coming to an end, but the uncertainty of the alien's true intentions and the dangers of traveling to another continent were equally untenable. Les knew that his mind had to rule over his heart; and that meant staying in Canada. He loved Melanie and wanted to be with her, but the thought of gallivanting around Columbia on a quest for an unknown farm seemed futile at best. If the United States was hostile, certainly a place like Columbia would be worse. He didn't sleep much that night; just listened to the uninterrupted rain pelting the roof and windows.

Melanie awoke early that morning and made coffee, which permeated through the cabin and into the bedroom. Les had finally gone to sleep, but opened his eyes as he smelled the brew. He joined her in the kitchen, red eyed from the endless night. "You look like hell, Les."

"I didn't sleep."

"She glanced out the window. "It's still raining. We have a lot of preparation. I got a friend in San Diego who can get us out the country safely. He can get us some passports and…" She noticed he was dejected. "Something wrong?"

"Yeah, there's something wrong."

"Les, there's nothing here for us. At least in Columbia we have a chance."

"Is this such a horrible place to live out our lives?"

She gulped the last of her coffee. "You're not going, are you?"

"I thought about it all night."

"If you stay, you'll die."

"And if I go we'll probably both die."

"You have to go, Les. I love you. I don't want to live without you."

"Then stay."

Tears began to glisten off the side of her eye ducts. "Please go with me?"

He couldn't remember an occasion when she had actually cried. "Mel, look at us. We're repeating our past behavior. We're in the same place we were so many years ago when you left me for the Extravaganza. It's becoming a pattern. Two people going their separate ways. Does it always have to end up this way?"

"It doesn't have to. My first decision was to leave the Bureau. This one is to leave the planet."

"It's the same thing, Melanie. And you know it."

Her tears flowed uncontrollably as she ran to the bedroom and shut the door. He had never seen her so vulnerable. He wandered into the bedroom and sat next to her as she sobbed. "You can choose differently this time. Make the choice for our relationship. For being together forever."

"No Les. I can't. I got to go."

Later in the day she began to pack her suitcase. There wasn't much conversation as Les took it upon himself to prepare what could be their last dinner together. Hardly a word was spoken between bites of the roasted turkey. They both realized that no matter what was going to happen, their relationship was coming to an end.

"I was thinking we'd go into town tomorrow and buy an SUV for me. You can keep the truck."

"Sure, that sounds fine."

She gazed around the room. 'This place is yours now."

"It's not going to be the same."

"There's still enough time to change your mind."

He hung his head low. "I'm not changing my mind."

Les couldn't even sleep in the bedroom with her that night. His soul ached for the woman he truly loved; one he would lose twice in a lifetime. The rain fell hard against the roof and the watery torrents swished rapidly through the gutters. In the morning there was a partial sun on the way into town where they purchased a new SUV. When they arrived back home she gathered her suitcase and packed it into the van.

"All there?"

"I have everything I need." She gazed upon him with downcast eyes. "Are you absolutely sure you won't go with me?"

"I'm going to put all my cards on the table. I once watched a show on adult male gray kangaroos. I'll never forget it; two big males fighting each other for the right to mate. They held onto each other's shoulders and took turns kicking each other in the stomach. They kicked each other for hours; each blow no harder than the other. But for some reason that one last kick ended the fight and the loser ran off. I bring up this story because I think it pertains to the earth now. Melanie, I'm afraid our kangaroo has been kicked." He leaned against the van. "Whether you're successful or not, I've found a home here. I don't want to leave."

"These aliens must be benevolent. And they have a purpose for the human race. I'm going to find out what that purpose is."

He embraced her so hard it almost cracked her ribs. "I love you, Melanie Blake. I'm going to miss you."

March 2021

A WHITE FROST SETTLED OVER the Canadian town and the cold air still required heavy coats and thick boots. Without a hint spring, Les Palmer kept his fire place burning and his scarf tightly around his neck. Since the months that Melanie had left, he had gradually found time to familiarize with the townsfolk, who knew him as James Dunston, retired computer expert. He was more than accommodating to his new friends that had complicated programming issues.

Les even gathered up the courage to date a woman who had inherited a local saloon from her father. She was strong willed, yet had the feminine qualities that Les found attractive. Her name was Mary and she had medium brown hair, an average figure and a sweet smile. She liked wearing jeans and was adored by everyone who had been raised in the town. Les admired her independence and confidence in life and Mary enjoyed his intellectual curiosity. They were as much friends as lovers and had free flowing conversations on a variety of mutual interests.

Mary was asleep next to Les in his cabin the when sunlight through the windows heated her eyelids. She stretched her arm over his chest. "Good morning, darling."

He snuggled up next to her. "Hey, is that sun?"

"Sure is. After a week's rain."

"Great." He stroked her hair. "Maybe we should mess around a little."

Her yawn turned into a smile, and then she gathered up the blanket and tossed it over his head.

He pulled it down and tickled her stomach and sides. She threw her pillow at him and then he pinned her down on the mattress. She giggled, and then they kissed passionately; spreading their hands across each other's warm skin.

After a few hours of making love and sprawling out lazily on the bed, Les got up and turned on the television set. The news anchor was in mid sentence. "...continues to be reports of radiation in the Mideast. There has been no official death toll. Russia has seized most of its former regions and seems in control of those territories. The President of the United States has been relocated to an unspecified place. Many sources have put that place in Tennessee, but we have no confirmation. As of now, the damage has been localized. The President's staff has assured us that he will return to Washington in the next few weeks. As of today, there have been no further biological attacks. The military has reported record enlistment. And if anyone still cares, Los Angeles continues to be a war zone." The anchor shuffled some papers and raised his eyebrows. "This just in. The remains of hotel financier Harry Philer was found in the desert the other day. It was mostly skeletal remains, but documents were found on him that verified his identification. As some may know, Philer was the owner and operator of the hotel Extravaganza in Nevada. Incidentally, the hotel has been enjoying its busiest season under new management." The anchor grinned enthusiastically. "Now on to the world of sports!"

Les turned off the television set. "I'm hungry. Let's eat."

"I'll cook a real country breakfast."

He ambled into the kitchen. "The news is becoming more depressing by the day."

"The world's always got problems."

"It doesn't seem to bother you that much, Mary."

"What can I do about it? What's going to happen is going to happen."

"Why don't you move in with me?"

She stopped stirring the scrambled eggs. "Really?"

"I'm serious. We're a perfect match. We should live together."

"That'd be fantastic. Are you sure?"

"I asked, didn't I? You're the most important person in my life and I think I'm falling in love with you."

"Les, I feel the same way."

"You live over your bar. You need a home."

She burned the eggs. "Oh crap. Well, I don't care. I'm just so happy."

He smiled. "We'll have cereal."

Later that evening the tavern was full of patrons celebrating Les and Mary's new arrangements. The juke box thumped out loud country rock music and the beer flowed as fast as Mary could pour it. Les sat at the end of the long counter among his new friends, who had known Mary most of their lives. They bashed their mugs together and cheerfully toasted the raucous party. Some danced between the tables and others rushed to the bathroom at regular intervals. One of the largest men in town, a lumberjack by trade, slapped his big paw on Les' shoulder.

"Hey, old buddy. You and Mary, huh?"

"Yes."

"I've known her since we were kids. You better treat her good."

"With friends like you, I'd better."

They both laughed aloud as a police officer sat down next to him. "I've known Mary since grade school."

"Cliff, she's told me you are one of her best friends."

Mary walked over to them. "Hey Cliff."

"You better watch this one. The ladies got an eye for him."

"I don't blame them. But he's mine." She pointed at the two imposing men. "Hey babe, these guys aren't giving you a hard time?"

"No. They're like my new big brothers."

"You know James, when we were kids Mary saved my life."

"Not that story, Cliff"

He sat up curiously. "No, tell me."

"We were at Klempers pond and I slipped through the ice. Mary pulled me out."

"I almost fell in after him."

Les finished his beer. "My hero."

"Think so?" A customer called out to her at the far end of the counter.

Cliff nodded at him. "You take care of her. She's special."

"I have to agree with you, there."

Mary returned with another beer for Les. "Don't get too drunk."

"Why, you're driving." He placed his arm around Cliff. "Mary, you got great friends. They really watch out for you."

Cliff chuckled. "Mary can handle herself, James. Believe me, she can out hunt and out fish all of us."

"I wouldn't go that far."

"You like hunting, James?"

"To be honest, I've never hunted before. But I have fished. I like that."

"Great, cause we got some good fishing up here."

Mary gestured for Les to follow her down the bar counter. "How are you doing, babe? My friends giving you the third degree?"

"No, they're fine. You didn't date any of them, did you? I don't want a four hundred pound lumberjack after my ass."

"I've dated. But nothing serious. You don't have any competition."

The party volume increased as the evening progressed past midnight. Mary called out one last round of drinks at 2:00 in the morning, but most had enough and were either asleep on the counter or singing nonsensical tunes. Although Cliff had partaken in more than a few alcoholic beverages, the other police officers were on hand to drive him or any other partygoers home. Les was feeling no pain, but Mary had remained the responsible hostess.

They locked up the saloon and Mary drove Les home and angled him towards the bedroom, where he immediately passed out on the mattress. She removed his shoes and draped a blanket over him. After shutting off all the lights and washing her face and brushing her teeth, she joined him in bed and fell asleep.

Les opened his eyes in the morning and winced from the pounding inside his head. Mary had already mixed an orange juice and vodka drink for his hangover. "What the hell happened last night?"

"You don't remember proposing to Cliff?"

"No way!"

"Just kidding. We all had a good time. You just had a little too much."

"You're telling me. I feel awful"

"Hey, drink this. You'll feel better."

"I don't want to be known as the town drunk."

"Don't worry. Harvey's got that over you."

Les wobbled into the living room and stared out at the front yard. "I've been meaning to build a picket fence around the place. Wouldn't that look great?"

She walked into the living room. "Sure. Can you do that kind of work?"

"I've never done it before. How hard can it be?"

"I've never done it before, either. But it looks hard."

Two weeks had passed without any significant world cataclysms and the temperatures were warming throughout western Canada. There were still small patches of snow, but an increasing growth of grass pushed up through the soil. Les kept busy repairing people's computers, but also found time to start designing his new picket fence. Using a three dimensional program, he was able to design several models that used different materials and structural styles. Mary was always supportive; even though she had doubts he could actually build a fence. But she did have a few friends in construction that were willing to help him.

Cliff arrived one morning to go fishing with Les.

Mary had purchased new curtains and furniture and was more than glad to get him out of the house for a while. The rivers had thawed and the fish were hungry. Les really enjoyed casting a line into the turbulent waters as the trout fought frantically over the bait. Les saw that Cliff, who at first seemed to be having fun, had become sullen. "What's the matter?"

"It's nothing."

"Come on, Cliff. Something's bothering you."

"It's this life up here. I love it so much. All of us do. I'm just not sure how long it's going to last."

Les put his fishing pole down. "What do you mean?"

"I grew up in this place. Some people moved away to city to make a new life. That's all right, I guess. But those that stayed like me and Mary; we love it here. I've been a police officer for ten years and folks are real. I fear some tyrant will take over the world, or the whole world will just blow itself up."

"I see. Well Cliff, the world's in deep shit. There's no way to sugar coat it. We can't change what's going to happen. We can only live day by day."

"I got family and friends."

"I understand your concern."

"Why can't mankind just stop killing each other?"

"There's the sixty four thousand dollar question. And I don't have a good answer. Greed. Avarice. Selfishness. Wasn't it Plato that once said that if we get something, we always want more?"

"I don't want more. Just what we have here."

Les picked up his rod and smiled. "Let's get back to catching fish."

They brought Mary home at least ten good size trout for a dinner. She insisted that Cliff join them and he happily complied. After dinner they huddled around the fireplace and told Les wonderful stories of their childhood where their backyards never seem to end. As Mary talked, Les admired her and knew he had finally found the real meaning of home.

The month of March was winding down and even though it was still cool, the leaves grew vibrantly green and the flowers began to unfold. Les finally decided to build the fence and went into town to get advice from the lumber yard proprietor. "Just remember to use redwood, James."

"You keep telling me that."

"You'll thank me in the winter."

"It just doesn't paint well."

"Maybe, but it looks manly."

"I guess I should think about weather."

"And don't you worry. Me and the boys will help you once you're ready."

"I appreciate that."

Les stopped at the saloon to visit Mary. She was in the office calculating the month's bills. He bent over and kissed her. "Just ordered the wood."

"Great."

"What time you coming home?"

She wiggled her eyebrows. "Why, what did you have in mind?"

"I always have that in mind. But I'm going to stop on the way home and get some ribs. We're barbecuing tonight."

"Sounds delicious."

"You still got the night off, right?"

"Nobody's keeping me here."

On the way home Les squinted from the sunlight twinkling through the majestic trees lining the side of the road. He listened to some rock music and when the news came on he scanned for a country music station. He turned up into his driveway, got out of the truck, grabbed the bundle of pork ribs and carried them up to the porch. Before entering the house, something caught his eye on the far end of the deck. He went over and picked up an eight by eleven manila folder with the name, 'Les Palmer' printed in large black letters. He held it up, jiggled it and felt something sliding around inside. He walked into the house, tore it open and held up a single unmarked computer disc.

Les brought it over to the computer on the roll up desk and inserted it. He was stunned to see Melanie Blake seated against a gray background. "Hello Les, I hope you are well. It was a difficult journey, but I made it to Columbia and I found the farm. Frederick Cabler eventually sold it to that farmer, who has owned it ever since. It was just by sheer chance that this farm was even selected. Frederick was the first in a line of humans, including Abel Crawley's family and then Abel Crawley himself to go away with them. Les, I was all wrong about these extraterrestrials. We had wondered if they were benevolent or malevolent. They were neither. And perhaps the saddest thing is that they didn't come to save our planet. They are caretakers of sorts for a very advanced non corporeal race that suffers a kind of senility in the latter days of their long existence. When this happens, they can no longer maintain their cohesiveness and require a much simpler way of life. These caretakers roam the universe for worlds that are about to destroy themselves. They are peaceful and do not instigate, nor rush the pace of a planet's destruction. Such is the fate of our planet. Much like those elderly aliens, we are at the end of our existence. These caretakers take some of us and use our genetic codes to reproduce fairly close facsimiles. They learn our way of life to prepare the way for the new tenants. I guess the good thing is that a few hundred of us or so get to live the remainder of our lives on other worlds. They do this because they lament the extinction of any species. In this they are kind, thoughtful. But I am the last and there will be no others. I'm sorry; sorry for the earth. Because I do love you and I will miss you. They reluctantly agreed to bring this recording to you before we left. I must go now, Les. I only wish they would have allowed you to come with us."

Body numb and his mind detached, Les watched clear footage of the now infamous farm where the trees seemed to be more overgrown than they had been in the 1968 film. Facing away from the camera, Melanie walked towards the eucalyptus trees, stopped and turned around. She was joined by the farmer and the sudden materialization of the saucer overhead. She waved to the camera and she and the farmer vanished, along with the saucer. The film ran for a few seconds longer and then went dark.

Les sat motionless for at least five minutes without blinking. He suddenly felt empty and without hope. As he bemoaned the loss of his doomed planet, Mary entered the living room with a wide and cheerful smile.

It was Mary that he truly loved and it took a moment like this to bring him out of despair and hopelessness. He ran over to her and hugged and kissed her enthusiastically.

"Wow! What did I do to deserve this?"

"You're the best."

"I thought you were more excited about the fence."

"Forget the fence. It's you I love."

"This is some greeting. Well, I love you too."

"Can't a man be thrilled to have his woman come home?"

"Absolutely. I'm not complaining."

Les got down on one knee and held her hands. "Mary, I want you to be my wife."

She was speechless. "You're serious."

"We love each other. I think it's perfect. Let's get married."

Her eyes glazed over with moisture. "Yes! Yes, I will marry you. Of course I will marry you."

"I want to spend the rest of my life with you."